Please return / renew by date shown.
You can renew it at:
norlink.norfolk.gov.uk
or by telephone: 0344 800 8006
Please have your library card & PIN ready

LOUD AND PROUD COLLECTION

NORFOLK LIBRARY
AND INFORMATION SERVICE

Visit us at www.boldstrokesbooks.com

A CLASS ACT

by

T. L. Hayes

2016

A CLASS ACT

ISBN 13: 978-1-62639-701-9

This Trade Paperback Original Is Published By
Bold Strokes Books, Inc.
P.O. Box 249
Valley Falls, NY 12185

First Edition: August 2016

___

CREDITS
EDITOR: RUTH STERNGLANTZ
PRODUCTION DESIGN: STACIA SEAMAN
COVER DESIGN BY MELODY POND

Acknowledgments

First and foremost, I would like to thank Sandy Lowe and Ruth Sternglantz from Bold Strokes Books. I appreciate the opportunity they have given me in publishing my first novel, and I hope to work with them again in the future. A special thanks to Ruth for all the creative ideas and for helping turn my often lackluster prose into, what I hope, is a very readable story.

Before this story was ever accepted for publication, it was in the hands of my three beta readers. I appreciated and incorporated as much of their advice as I could. I fully believe that the eventual acceptance of the manuscript was due in large part to their advice, though I'm sure you'll notice that the finished product looks much different from the story you first read. So thank you: Julie Davis, Diane Karns, and Crystal Zachary. I couldn't have done it without you.

I owe much debt to my mentor, Dr. Ren Draya, head of the English Department at Blackburn College. Not only did she help mold me into the writer I am today, but was most helpful with this project by providing me with research materials concerning how a college would handle the situation described in this book. Any realism on that subject is due to the material she provided me with. Any surrealism on that subject is due to my own shortcomings.

Any time I came upon a situation wherein I had to ask myself, "What would a real professor do in that situation?" I went to one person: Dr. Lara LaDage, assistant professor of biology at Penn State Altoona, and a dear friend. I appreciate all of your insights and the often as not, shared laugh.

A very special thank you to my writing buddy and close friend, April Duncan. Though we have yet to collaborate on a project together, (who knows, maybe someday), she has been such a big supporter and motivator all through this process. She has been my cheerleader, she has been my harshest critic, and she has been an inspiration. Thank you so much, my friend.

And last, thank you to Jaykob Hayes, my husband, my supporter in every possible way. Yet another writing project that saw me chained to my desk and letting the house go. Thank you for picking up the slack, as always, and for making it possible for me to do this by being the only one in the house with a job.

My Mother's Voice

To speak in her voice
A child's dream
The art of imitation
Is a flattery that
Takes work.
It's not a perfect match
At nine I knew
How everyone asked for them—
I wanted that too.
I tried to recreate
With a pencil on fat-lined paper
But nothing would come.
When I picked up the pen again
I wrote stories
Not like her
My language was different
But I didn't stop trying
To speak.

T. L. Hayes

Chapter One

The end of August in the Midwest was still blazing hot and humid, so by the time Rory Morgan arrived at Roberts Hall, the main academic building for the theater department, she was drenched in sweat, and her long, curly red hair was damp and starting to frizz a little. The backpack slung over her shoulder didn't help matters, adding extra heat. She was sure she looked like a mess—she definitely felt like one.

When she walked into the classroom for her Topics in Theater class, there weren't many open desks left. She only saw one person she knew, Davis, but there were no open seats near him, so she made her way to a seat in the middle of the third row, behind a blonde with an open laptop on her desk, who was texting on her phone. She sat, unpacked her binder and a pen, and stretched her long legs out in front of her, trying not to kick the blonde's feet in the process.

She was looking forward to the class with Dr. Parks. Rory had never taken a class with her before as an undergraduate but knew she taught a few required grad school classes, such as Stage Combat, which she was looking forward to. She and her best friend Rachel planned to take that class together so, as Rachel claimed, they could beat the snot out of each other.

She had heard Parks was a hard grader who expected a lot from her students and who could be hard to please. Rory figured taking this class—a cross-listed upper-level undergrad elective and introductory grad course—would prepare her for the tougher classes later on. Rory took the reviews of the other students in stride. She figured a lot of the negativity probably stemmed from students who were just pissed that they had to actually work for a change. She got tired of hearing students bitch and moan when they heard they had to write a fifteen-page paper or that Wikipedia wasn't a real source. What did they think college was about? She, for one, was not there to party, despite Rachel's constant attempts to drag her out.

She wasn't sure what she expected Dr. Parks to look like, but the small woman who walked in a few minutes later, wearing a white pantsuit with a black blouse, her jacket unbuttoned and the sleeves rolled up, and her brown hair pulled back in a tight French braid that went all the way down her back, with wire-framed glasses over her dark brown eyes, wasn't it. Rory thought she looked too adorable to be someone who could kick anyone's butt, even if it was in the simulated world of stage combat. Rory smirked. Hard grader—she looked like an elf. A really, adorable elf. Kind of cute, really.

Dr. Parks put the items she had brought with her on the desk at the front of the room and smiled at her students. "Good afternoon. For those of you who don't know me, I'm Dr. Margaret Parks. And for those of you who do"—she gave a stern, yet playful look to Davis and a few others—"I am also known as She Who Must Be Obeyed." Some of the students only laughed nervously or gave a wan smile, but Rory and Davis laughed appreciatively.

Rory mentally chastised her classmates. *That was funny.*

Then, Dr. Parks smiled. "No, I'm not really that mean, right, Davis?"

Pretending to look scared, Davis said, "No, ma'am, not at all. Tame as a kitten, you are."

Dr. Parks nodded in his direction. "Thank you, Davis, that was lovely."

Rory was enjoying the show, thinking she was also going to enjoy the class, regardless of whatever was on the syllabus. She reappraised Dr. Parks. She chuckled to herself when the thought came to her that the professor was dressed like the cover of Michael Jackson's *Thriller* album and hoped it wasn't on purpose. At the same time, however, she saw fierceness there. It came out in the way the woman moved about the room, with her hands casually in her pockets, as she discussed what they would be learning that semester. Rory had barely registered that and gave a vague response earlier when she had been called upon to introduce herself, because she had been too busy watching Dr. Parks to pay much attention. She hadn't realized it was possible to be adorable and fierce at the same time, but this woman had no trouble pulling it off. When Dr. Parks smiled, one corner of her mouth rose in such a way that it looked as if she was teasing or in a playful mood, and her eyes seemed to spark with what Rory could only call mischief.

Rory realized with a start that she was attracted to this woman and that came as a surprise. Dr. Parks was not like any of the girls she had been attracted to before. In the past, she had mainly been attracted to girls she thought of as intellectual butches, young women much like her: young, smart, and butch. She always fell for good conversationalists who could challenge her on any given topic and who were not slaves to fashion and makeup. But the butch she had in her head as being her ideal didn't seem to exist anymore. She really loved the butches from previous generations who had short DA haircuts, leather jackets, clunky boots, and a bad attitude—but a heart of gold. That kind of butch was disappearing, however, and being replaced with the metrosexual, hipster butches who thought nothing of pairing a well-tailored suit with makeup. This, to her, was just so much blasphemy.

The butches she admired and wanted to date were also the type of butch she wanted to be. She admired their swagger and their comfort with themselves and the world around them, even when the world wasn't comfortable with them. It was the tough attitude that she really wanted, though, without seeming like a sexist asshole.

All that being said, her sudden attraction to Dr. Parks confused her. Dr. Parks wasn't butch at all, nor was she really a femme. Rory was going to call simply academic: respectable, but sexless. Not to say the *professor* was sexless, just that her clothing did not give any clue as to her sexual orientation, nor did it aim to attract.

I must be losing my mind, she thought. How old was the prof, anyway? She looked to be in her early to mid-forties, though it was hard to say for sure. She had never been attracted to older women before. She didn't have any hang-ups about it; it had just never come up. But she couldn't take her mind off the adorable, fierce woman.

❖

Travel coffee mug in one hand and a stack of syllabuses and pens in the other, Margaret Parks headed to the classroom at the end of the hall. It was her last class of the day and she hoped she could keep them awake. The class started at three and, over the years, she had noticed by that time of day many students seemed to need a nap. Either that or she was just boring. But morning classes were no better, as the students were barely awake, and many were still hungover from the night before. Plus, she hated the casualness that had taken hold over the last few years. Some students, girls mostly, she noticed, had started to come to class wearing slippers and pajama pants, not even trying to get dressed, which she found rude. She almost wished she could ban sleepwear from her classroom, even though she knew it made her sound like a fuddy-duddy.

When she walked into her classroom, nearly every desk was full. She expected that by the next class some of those desks would be empty, as there were always students who dropped out by then. Even though it was a cross-listed class for seniors and grad students, she knew she only had two grad students: Davis Zachary and Aurora Morgan. Davis, she knew, as she'd had him in several classes and had directed him twice in past productions. Aurora Morgan was unknown to her, however, so she knew nothing of what the girl looked like or what kind of student she was.

She kept the introductions brief—she knew everyone hated them. "Okay, we're going to go around the room. You can introduce yourself as you wish to be addressed, and I will make every effort to remember your chosen name and respect it. Davis, you start. Sound off." Margaret smiled at him, crossed her arms in front of her chest, and leaned against her desk.

"Zachary, Davis. First year MFA. I prefer Davis, thank you." Davis gave a winning smile and everyone laughed.

The introductions continued around the room, until they reached the redhead in the third row. "Aurora Morgan. You can call me Rory." That was it, simple and to the point.

Margaret nodded. "Nice to meet you, Rory." The girl instantly blushed and Margaret tried not to smile or indicate she had noticed. She wasn't sure what would make the girl blush so easily, as she had barely said anything to her. Out of the corner of her eye, she noticed the girl was watching her intently as she began to walk about the room. In her experience, students only paid that close attention for one of two reasons: either they really were interested in the lecture or they were interested in you. Considering she wasn't lecturing, she figured it was the latter, but she wasn't sure why. Was she the only interesting thing to look at in the room?

What would Rory see in her? Student crushes were a reality of teaching; they just happened. She'd had her fair share as a student and nothing ever came of them. Since she had become a professor, there had been a few students over the years who she was aware of who had crushed on her, who always made themselves known by their furtive glances, easy blushes, and always seeking her out for special attention. She tried to treat them all with respect but not encourage them, either. As the years went on and she got older and gray started to creep into her hair, the crushes had started to taper off. Which was more than fine with her. Dealing with the unwanted attention that could come when the campus at large thought a teacher was dating a student, whether warranted or not, was not something she wanted to deal with.

When she dated, which was rare, it was always a woman her own age. So even if this child was interested in her, she knew enough to stay away from the mess that could create. *Focus, Parks, back to reality.*

Once the introductions were over, she announced, "Oh, for those of you who are interested, I will be directing a play this semester, *Cat on a Hot Tin Roof*, and I urge you to try out. And if you're not an actor, that's okay. We need behind-the-scenes people as well. You can see me after class for more information. Okay, back to the matter at hand."

❖

Rory knew that she was going to try out. How could she not? If Dr. Parks was directing that would mean more time with the woman. Rory was suddenly curious about what she would be like as a director. She'd only worked on a few productions since coming to college, each with a different director, and they had all been different. She had a feeling Dr. Parks would be interesting to watch, which she was becoming very good at as it was. *Careful, Morgan, she's going to catch you staring. Don't be a creeper. Don't be a creeper.*

Once class was over, everyone filed out except Rory and Davis, both of whom went up to the big desk.

Davis smiled at Rory. "Hey, baby girl, how was your summer?"

"Good. Boring. I was my dad's cheap help, as always." Her father was a lawyer and she spent every summer doing odd jobs for him around the office, anything from fetching coffee, to making copies, to running errands. The money she made was what she lived on during the school year.

Dr. Parks was smiling at them and didn't interrupt as they briefly caught up. After a moment, she said, "So, you two brave souls want to try out?"

"Uh, duh!" Davis said. "You know if you're directing, I'm there."

Laughing, Dr. Parks said, "Thank you, Davis. I'm always glad to see you there." She turned to Rory. "What about you, Ms. Morgan? Will you be auditioning?"

"Yes, ma'am." She gave the woman her best smile.

"Excellent! I know Davis's work, but I can't say that I know yours."

Before Rory could speak, Davis said, "I know I'm a great actor and you must have been so mesmerized by my singing in *Rent* that you missed Miss Thing over here strutting her stuff as the fabulous free spirit Maureen."

Dr. Parks looked somewhat shocked and embarrassed at the same time and she briefly covered her mouth. "Oh my God, I'm so sorry. I didn't recognize you. You were wonderful. And your voice is amazing."

Rory gave her a sheepish grin and said, "Thanks."

"Now I just wish I was directing a musical."

"Maybe next time."

Holding her gaze for a moment, Dr. Parks said, "Yeah, maybe."

Davis coughed. "So, where and when, Doc?"

Dr. Parks broke eye contact with Rory to glare at Davis. "Nowhere, if you call me *Doc* again." Then she smiled.

"Yeah, yeah." Davis gifted her with a big grin.

Dr. Parks turned to Rory and shook her head. "Impertinent child. Anyway, auditions start Friday in Maguire Hall, room 200."

"Sweet. I'll be there," Rory said.

"Great." Dr. Parks suddenly gave Rory a concerned look. "Now, I just want to make sure you're going to have the time. You're a first-year grad student, right?"

"Right."

"Your mandatory acting hours won't come up until later in the program, so I just want to be sure that with a full load, you would be able to devote as much time to this as I'd need you to."

"How much time are we talking?"

"Well, rehearsals are Thursdays, Fridays, and Saturdays, at least four hours a day."

"Sounds good. I got the time."

"I know some students also like to have fun on the weekends"—without taking her eyes off Rory, she gave an obvious nod in Davis's direction—"and like to have all the free time they can get."

"What can I say?" Davis retorted. "I am a rainbow-colored social butterfly and sometimes I must fly."

Rory thought Davis was pretty fierce in his own right and his theatrics made her smile. "Well, I, on the other hand, have no use for a social life, and I can make it. I'm all yours." Rory hoped she wasn't turning red.

❖

When class was over and everyone started to file out, only two students, Rory and Davis, came up to inquire about the play. Margaret smiled at their easy light banter. Since this was the first time she had seen Rory standing up, she hadn't realized how tall the girl was. Margaret had to look up at her, but that was all right. Up close, she could see just how attractive Rory was. Despite the long hair, Margaret read her as a butch: the clunky boots and big leather belt, holding up faded blue jeans, the plain white T-shirt, the style of her walk, the way she carried herself, the lack of makeup...not that she needed any. Rory reminded her of a young Julia Roberts, if Julia Roberts had been born a butch lesbian, as she suspected Rory was. She bit her lip to suppress a smile, at the same time telling herself she had no right to be pleased at that thought.

Rory's response to her question about the rehearsal schedule caught her off guard. "I'm all yours." Immediately upon saying it, the girl had blushed and averted her eyes.

This was going to be interesting. Margaret tried not to smirk, as Rory's attention actually flattered her, no matter how much she kept telling herself to just ignore it. There was no denying the girl was gorgeous. Improper or not, she'd be lying if she said she didn't notice.

As Rory and Davis left the room, she had to force herself not to watch the girl leave. *What the hell's the matter with you?*

she mentally scolded herself. She did not ogle her students. She wasn't one of those professors. *Stop being a lech!* She gave them a couple of minutes to clear the hallway then she too left and went back to her office, still wondering at her sudden attraction and what it meant. It meant she needed to get laid—by someone her own age.

CHAPTER TWO

Rory came into class on that Wednesday, jamming on her iPod to one of her favorites, "When Love Comes to Town," off U2's *Rattle and Hum*, featuring the incomparable B.B. King. One of her undergrad roommates had teased her about her music because she didn't listen to anything recorded past the turn of the current century. No one really sang anymore since the invention of Auto-Tune, plus all the music sounded the same to her. There didn't seem to be a lot of variation in rhythm and tempo. That same roommate had accused her of being old. She had countered that she just had good taste. She and that roommate never did become friends.

After she had set down and pulled her books out of her bag, she kept the beat with her pen and had her eyes closed, enjoying it. She had to restrain herself from going all out and playing air drums or guitar. She had the volume down low so she'd hear when Dr. Parks came in—she didn't want to get in trouble. Plus, she wanted to hear everything that woman had to say.

When Dr. Parks came in, she smiled at everyone and Rory quickly took her earbuds out and stashed her music in her backpack. Based on the syllabus, the first couple of weeks were going to be old info for her, and she knew she could zone out if she wanted to. But she didn't want to. She found Dr.

Parks fascinating. Rory spent her time studying her professor. She had a habit of pacing back and forth in front of the class while she talked with her hands in her pockets. It was when she took off her glasses and rubbed her eyes that Rory saw her vulnerability. With her glasses off, Dr. Parks looked tired and like she could use a break.

Rory had felt a strong pull toward Dr. Parks on that first day of class, a pull that she hadn't felt toward anyone before. Not that she hadn't had crushes on girls before, but this was different. Growing up, she had kept her nose in her books and tried to pretend the rest of the world didn't exist. She had known she was gay from a young age, back in grade school. When she got to high school, she decided that she was not going to date guys just to appear straight; she came out. Not that anyone seemed to notice, except her parents, that is, who told her it was okay and they still loved her, that nothing would change that.

When she got to college she knew she wasn't the only gay person on campus but she hadn't found anyone she was willing to date more than twice. She put all of her focus into her studies. True, Rachel had wanted to date, but Rory just didn't return her feelings. After the wrap party for *Rent*, they had ended up dancing and making out, but Rory blamed it on the beer. Rachel took the rejection well and had since become her best friend.

She wondered if she would ever have the courage to ask Dr. Parks out. Should she dare? What if she got turned down? What if she got turned down and then things got awkward? What if the professor said yes, but then it all went to hell and *then* it got awkward?

In other words, most scenarios she could imagine ended with it getting awkward.

What if the professor wasn't even gay? She surely wasn't giving off any signs either way, not that Rory was an expert. She didn't know what to look for. And if Dr. Parks wasn't gay, she might be offended at the implication. But, she reasoned, she wasn't going to know unless she took the plunge, stopped second-guessing herself, and just did it. And she knew that if she didn't do it now, she might never do it. Well, not *now* in the middle of class, but after class for sure. She just had to figure out what to say.

She had little experience asking anyone out. She had been asked out several times, but mostly by guys and they were all horrible. Each time, she had to tell herself not to laugh in his face. Her most recent hopeful had been Chad, the student worker who pulled the night shift at the front desk of her dorm. Chad was an okay guy and they had a love/hate camaraderie that worked well. He had initially tried to use humor to ask her out. One night when she had come back from working late in the library he had called out to her from his perch behind the front desk.

"Hey, Ginger. You wanna help me get off my island?"

Amused more than flattered or offended, she walked up to the desk and said, "No, little buddy, I think you need to stay where you are."

"Aww, that's not nice."

"And don't call me Ginger. It's not even accurate."

"So would you go out with me if I called you a redhead?"

"Chad, I wouldn't go out with you if you called me Your Highness and kissed my feet."

"You know, a less cultured guy than myself would have sneered and called you a derogatory name by now. Perhaps even suggested that you don't even like guys."

She'd leaned in as if to impart a secret. "If a girl is a

lesbian because she doesn't want to go out with you, then this campus must be dyke central. A girl can dream. Good night, Chad." She'd given him a little wave.

Chad had called after her, "Was that supposed to hurt me, pointing out what I already know? You might as well have also called me a white guy. A devastatingly handsome white guy."

Rory shook herself out of her reverie. She started to think about the whole asking Dr. Parks out and it getting awkward thing. Not only did they see each other in class twice a week, but if she was cast in the play, they would be seeing each other outside of class as well. Rory would get to be in the same room with Dr. Parks, and that prospect held a lot of potential for awkwardness. She realized that now was not the best time to just charge up to the woman and ask her out. It was best to take her time and get to know her better and see how things turned out. Maybe if she spent that much time with her she would be able to figure out if her professor was even gay or not.

On Friday, with her backpack slung over one shoulder and dressed in her usual uniform of boot-cut jeans, a white men's V-neck, and engineer boots, Rory walked into room 200 in Maguire Hall a few minutes early. Room 200 was a large open space with desks strewn about in a haphazard array. The room was often used for auditions and rehearsals. At one of the desks sat Dr. Parks with her head bent over some papers on a clipboard. She looked up when Rory walked in and she smiled. There were already several students waiting in a disjointed line and Rory took her place among them, leaned her back against the wall, put her hands behind her back, and propped up one boot-clad foot.

She had tried out for many roles since she had come to college but had been told by many directors that she just didn't have the look they were going for. Apparently, they hadn't been able to see past her cultivated butch image. She was a proud dyke and wasn't going to conform to convention, even if it cost her roles. Besides, lately she had been thinking that, though she loved acting, her future would best be spent backstage, maybe as a stage manager or a director. She wanted to be the one to bring great theater to life. Maybe even write some. She kept auditioning because she firmly believed in something her favorite undergrad professor, Dr. Baskin, had always said: Do as many jobs in the theater as you can, not only so you can know everything about how theater works, but also so that you can know where *you* work best.

❖

Margaret had chosen room 200 as the audition space because she wanted to be closer to her actors, it was that simple. Her approach to production had always been to build unity with her cast. Once a play was cast, she would have her cast perform a variety of team and intimacy building exercises that might look strange to an outsider. For instance, when she had directed *Romeo and Juliet* three years ago, she had her leads do an intimacy exercise where they sat on the floor facing each other, legs crossed, knees touching. They had to sit that way for five minutes, not saying a word, just looking into each other's eyes. These kinds of exercises were essential for building intimacy between actors who were supposed to be portraying characters who were in love. She wanted them to connect with each other. With this production, however, there was such a disconnect between the main characters in *Cat on a Hot Tin Roof* that an intimacy exercise would not be necessary.

Mark, the first student to read for Brick, practically lisped and sashayed as he read; she was livid and couldn't contain herself.

"Stop! What do you think you're doing?"

"Well, Brick is gay, right? I was just trying to make that come across."

She slowly set her pen down and took a moment before she looked back up. She was trying to get ahold of her anger. When she looked back up at the boy, she spoke in an even tone. "First of all, the fact of his homosexuality is not supposed to be readily apparent to the audience. But most importantly, not every gay man talks that way. Your portrayal is offensive and not what this play is about. Now, if you want to try reading normally, go on. Otherwise, we're done."

He thought about it a moment, then shrugged his shoulders and left. As she watched him leave, she saw Rory trying to suppress a grin. The girl was biting her lip in an effort to keep herself in check.

Next to read for Brick was Davis. As Margaret expected, he did a great job and she couldn't help but smile and nod and put a check mark next to his name. When all the guys had finished reading for Brick, she made her next announcement. "Okay, next, I want to have everyone who's reading for Maggie."

The first girl to read for the part read as if she was Marilyn Monroe having an asthma attack. It was unintentionally funny and Margaret did her best to hide a smile behind her fist, as she looked down at the paper in front of her and drew a line through the girl's name, then wrote in the margin, "Good-bye, Norma Jean," and chuckled to herself. When the girl was finished, she told her thanks and said, "Rory, your turn."

The tall redhead threw her backpack off to the side, then walked back to the center of the open area and stood just a few feet in front of Margaret. Just her mere presence was captivating. She just had a way of drawing your attention without even trying. Between her height, her hair, and her casual, cocky butch persona, Margaret couldn't take her eyes off her. She liked how Rory looked directly at her as she delivered her monologue, as if she were Brick. The girl had chosen to speak without a Southern accent but that didn't make her presentation any less effective. She still spoke with passion and intensity. She knew instantly that Rory would nail this role, accent or no.

When Rory was finished, Margaret couldn't say anything for a moment. While she collected herself, she put a check mark next to Rory's name and in all caps, "HER!" Then she looked up and said, "Thank you, Rory, that was wonderful. I do have to ask—why didn't you read it with an accent?"

"Because I suck at them."

Everyone in the room, including Margaret, laughed.

"Well, I appreciate your honesty. In truth, I think you reading the role in your own voice lent your delivery authenticity. Good job. Next." She watched as Rory retrieved her backpack and headed out the door. It didn't escape her notice that the blond girl in line gave Rory a nod that Rory seemed to pointedly ignore. She saw the predatory look on the blonde's face and didn't have to wonder at that. Rory was a beautiful girl and it was no wonder that she would attract a lot of attention. Even her own, apparently, she thought. But in her defense, she knew enough to stay away. Getting close to fires like that only left one burned, and Margaret knew when to back away from flames when they were too hot.

❖

"So, tell me about your latest mounting, Madam Director." Bill brought Margaret a glass of wine as she reclined on his couch in his living room after the first day's auditions. He parked his six-foot frame next to her. Bill, a departmental colleague, and his husband were her dearest friends. She and

Maxine had spent many nights at their apartment playing cards and drinking copious amounts of wine. When Maxine had left, Bill and Dix were the only two in their friends' circle who hadn't shut her out. Everyone else thought she had been wrong for choosing tenure over Maxine and had either made their opinions known about it or had just stopped calling her entirely. Which was fine with her, as Bill and Dix had always been her two favorite people. Now, sitting on their very comfy couch, with one leg tucked under her and her arm resting on the back, she smiled at Bill as he sat down next to her. Dix was still teaching so it was just the two of them.

"You make it sound so dirty."

"Oh, honey, if you do it right, theater is always dirty, even when it's tragic."

"Everything is always about sex with you people, isn't it?" Margaret quipped.

"And everything is always about drama with you lesbians, isn't it?"

Margaret sighed. "Can't argue with you there. Sex and drama are the same thing, right?"

"Only for your kind."

"Oh yes, I keep forgetting that gay men have no drama when it comes to sex."

"Oh, we do, it just doesn't stop us. Besides, sex shouldn't be so complicated. Speaking of which, when was the last time you had a little uncomplicatedness in your life?" Bill grinned at her and nudged her knee with his foot.

"You know when."

"My God, that conference was almost two years ago. You need to do something about that, or Miss Sassy is going to shrivel up and fall off."

Margaret couldn't help but laugh at his name for her clit.

The conference in question had been a one-night stand. She had allowed herself to be picked up in the hotel bar, and the woman in question, a theater professor from a school on the West Coast, had been quite attractive and rather insistent. It had been fun but neither had felt compelled to trade contact information and they'd left things with a handshake in Denver. "I hope you're wrong about that, but I do know that it's affecting me in other ways."

"Oh, do tell."

She knew Bill was the only person she could say things like this to. Not only was he her closest friend, but he could keep his mouth shut. She took a gulp of her wine, and then she said, "I've recently noticed how attractive one of my students is." She immediately felt embarrassed and hid her face on her arm on the back of the couch.

"Oh my God, you seriously need to get laid. You leave those Lolitas alone, they're nothing but trouble. I don't care how pert her breasts are or how nubile she is, just back away. Back away! Danger!"

Margaret laughed. "Calm down, I haven't done anything. I just said she's attractive. I think I'm going through a midlife crisis or something—I've never noticed girls half my age before."

"Well, that's always possible. You are the right age for that sort of thing." She looked at him agape and smacked his leg. "What? I'm just saying that this is the perfect time for you to have a midlife crisis—just keep it out of your classroom."

"Don't worry about that. I'm a good girl."

"Yeah, Eliza Doolittle said the same thing, but look how she turned out."

"Hey, all she did was fall in love with the rich guy."

"Yeah, and not her teacher." Bill gave her a pointed look.

"Don't worry about that. I have no delusions about that, I was just trying to say that this kid's been the only person I've even remotely noticed in a while. And I know how sad that is."

"That's because you don't go anywhere besides work and home, home and work. You need to get out more. Live a little."

"Oh yes, I keep forgetting all the opportunities there are in this town for lesbian hookups."

"Well, I hear they bowl." Bill snickered as Margaret slapped him on the arm.

"Do I really look like someone who bowls?"

"No, you're not butch enough for that."

"Exactly."

"Maybe you should go up to Chicago, visit some bars. I hear that's where the Midwest keeps their best lesbians."

"I'll keep that in mind."

"Trying to get you away from campus is like trying to get me to a Garth Brooks concert. But I digress."

"What, you don't like cowboys in tight jeans?"

"Oh, I do, just not the whiny sort, especially when they're whining about women. Gag me. Besides, I'm not supposed to be looking anymore." A contented smile spread across his face.

Margaret returned his smile. "See, that's what I want, someone who smiles like that when they think of me. I'm really not interested in cheap encounters. I want it to mean something."

Bill made a sound. "Lesbians! You disgust me."

❖

By the end of Saturday's auditions, Margaret had the play cast. It was no question that Rory and Davis were going to be the leads; they were the best by a long shot. She had sent emails to everyone who got a part and reminded them about rehearsals the following week. She knew the play was going to go well with those two leading it.

After her conversation with Bill Friday night, she felt a little foolish. Not for admitting to him she was attracted to a student, but for feeling it in the first place. Maybe Bill was right, and she just needed to get laid by someone her own age. Where to find such a woman, that was the question. The town she had been calling home for the last six years was not exactly a hotbed of lesbian activity. The only ones she knew were connected to her job, and she had already burned her bridges there with Maxine.

She supposed she could try online dating; she had heard it wasn't as scary as it used to be. But she wanted to make a real connection with someone and she worried she wouldn't be able to do that over the Internet. She wanted to look into the eyes of another woman and see her heart and her soul. She wanted to lay herself bare for that special someone and have that someone be able to do the same with her. She knew she was a romantic and perhaps old-fashioned, but she just wanted to be in love. She wanted someone to sweep her off her feet. She wanted someone who couldn't stand to be away from her for very long. She wanted a grand adventure. She just didn't see one happening anytime soon.

She sat at her desk at home, in the corner of her living room, musing. She chuckled to herself when she realized that she had something in common with the affable Charlie Brown: she too seemed to have a thing for an unobtainable redhead. She guessed that made Bill her Lucy. *I owe him a nickel.*

❖

Saturday evening, Rory was in her room, checking her email before she left for the evening. She was allowing Rachel to drag her out of her room for a bit of girls' night in, as Rachel called it. All that meant was she had invited some girls over to sit around and get drunk and laugh hysterically at nothing in particular. She sighed. It wasn't that she didn't like them; she just had little in common with them. Sure, they were all gay, so there was that, but that was about it. They didn't seem that much different than the straight girls Rory knew. They were just a bunch of giggling girls, talking about who they wanted to sleep with. Not her cup of tea.

Even though Rachel wasn't much different than the giggling girls sometimes, they had bonded and become close. Rachel was like a kid sister to her now, though they were the same age and she knew Rachel would have been more than happy to get out of the friend zone. But she respected the boundaries Rory had put in place. She flirted occasionally, but she always did it as a joke, knew when to back off, and was never blatant or pathetic about it.

Rory saw the email from Dr. Parks and opened it with anticipation.

Cast,

That's right, if you are receiving this email that means you have been cast in this year's production of *Cat on a Hot Tin Roof.* Congratulations! I will be expecting to see all of you every Thursday and Friday, from four p.m. to whenever I decide to release you, probably seven or so, and Saturdays, from eleven a.m. to ? The cast list is below. Contact me if you have questions.

Dr. Parks

Rory couldn't believe she got the part. Maggie the cat! Apparently not being able to do a Southern accent hadn't mattered. She grinned when she noticed that Miranda, a flirty blonde she'd been in a few undergrad classes with and who wouldn't take no for an answer, had been cast as May, the gold-digging daughter-in-law. It would be fun, she thought, to play opposite Davis. Though they had acted together before, they had never played opposite each other. He was more than a worthy actor. Rory almost wished Brick spoke more, because Davis deserved to shine, but, she mused, there were some quite dramatic scenes between Brick and Big Daddy that she knew Davis would excel at. The truth was, *Cat* was really a vehicle for the actor cast as Maggie, as she did most of the talking and was the spark that lit the fuse for the showdown scenes between Brick and his father. It was a big load to carry, but Rory was excited.

There was a knock on her unlocked door, and then Rachel walked in. Rachel had carte blanche to enter her room and did so quite frequently.

"Hey, Merida, let's go. Time to chill."

Rory leveled her gaze at Rachel. "I am *not* a princess, thank you very much." She began to close out her email and shut down her laptop.

"Aw, someone get up on the wrong side of the castle today?"

Rachel ruffled Rory's curls and Rory growled at her. Rachel laughed.

"I was in a fine mood, until you got here."

"Ouch. Sorry, love. You know I'm just playing. Don't be mad, pookie." Then, unprompted, Rachel began to sing a bit of Merida's song. Rachel was good, but Rory was better and she couldn't help but laugh and put her hands up in surrender. "All right, all right, stop, you're making my ears bleed. Besides, I have some news."

"What, Your Rudeness?"

Ignoring her, Rory couldn't contain her smile as she said, "Guess who just got the role of Maggie in *Cat*?"

"OMG, that's awesome!"

Rachel was the only person Rory knew who sometimes spoke out loud in chat-speak. She found it annoying, usually. This time she chose to ignore it. "I know. And Davis will be my husband."

Rachel deadpanned, "Wow, Davis playing a repressed gay man, what a stretch."

"Be nice."

"I am nice, I was just teasing. Actually, that's going to be a good show. Congrats." Rachel tugged on Rory's arm as Rory stood up from her chair. "Now come on, you're going to leave this room, if I have to drag you kicking and screaming."

Rory allowed herself to be pulled, but only just. "You and what army?"

Rachel stopped abruptly and this threw Rory off balance and she almost fell into Rachel, who was nice enough to catch her. "Oh, you're going to be like that, are you?"

"I am." They each crossed their arms across their chests and pretended to stare each other down. Rory always won these contests. She grinned. "I win, shorty, as usual. Now let's go. Throw me to the lions if you must."

"I think you mean lesbians, and if that's the case, I should dip you in honey first."

As they were walking out the door, Rory asked, "Be realistic. Where are you going to get that much honey this time of night?"

CHAPTER THREE

Rory's week became divided in her head between days she got to see Dr. Parks, and days she didn't. She spent her time in class alternating between trying to concentrate on the lecture and occasionally actually learning something, and just watching Dr. Parks. She was definitely not one of those professors who stood at a lectern, nor was she one of those professors who rounded everyone up in a circle and sat among them. Rory actually liked that approach for some classes, especially classes that involved a lot of creativity and exchanging of ideas. For lecture classes, however, Rory liked to be fixed in place so she could concentrate. Normally that wasn't a problem for her, but now, as she watched Dr. Parks casually pace in front of the class, often with her hands in her pockets and an animated smile on her lips, she couldn't swear that she had picked up all the finer points of the lecture.

As she was following her movements, hoping she didn't look like a starstruck groupie, Rory couldn't help but wonder again about this sudden attraction. Dr. Parks was not the type of woman she was normally attracted to. Dr. Parks's wardrobe seemed to consist of conservative and boring—and, sadly, sexless, in Rory's opinion—slacks and blouses, with the occasional blazer thrown in for a look of sass. Even so, Rory thought she was cute as hell. Cute, though not always the best word to compliment someone, seemed to be the best choice for Dr. Parks.

Rory also found herself mesmerized by the length of Dr. Parks's hair. Rory guessed the professor was around five feet tall, and her hair reached just beyond her waist and was held in place by a tight, compact braid. Rory found herself staring at it every time Dr. Parks turned around, and she wondered what it looked like when it was loose. She could easily envision herself running her fingers through it, could see the light catching the few strands of silver. She could see her hand gliding down to Dr. Parks's throat, caressing, while her lips followed, trailing kisses down her neck.

Startling herself by the vivid imagery, Rory immediately drew her legs up, sat up straight, and coughed a little, trying to bring herself back to the present. Her boots made a loud shuffling noise on the tile and several people looked curiously in her direction, including Dr. Parks. She smiled sheepishly and hoped she wasn't turning red, though she could feel her cheeks getting warm and knew she was giving herself away. She hated her pale complexion. Her cheeks were really good at letting everyone know when she was overheated or embarrassed, as she could hide nothing when the blush rose on her cheeks.

Margaret had been startled out of her lecture by the loud clunking of Rory's boots. It sounded as if the girl had almost fallen asleep and then jerked herself awake. As she walked up to Rory's desk to lightly tease her about the noise, she couldn't help but notice the color rising on her cheeks and thought that she had been right, that the girl had almost fallen asleep and was now embarrassed about being caught.

Margaret gave her a curious smile. "Everything okay, Rory?"

Rory returned her smile. "Yeah, I'm good. Sorry, I was just…my foot fell asleep. Had to move it."

"Well, I'm sorry I'm boring it. I'll try to be more entertaining." Everyone chuckled. "Anyway, as I was saying…"

As she got on with her lecture, in the back of her mind, she couldn't help thinking and wondering about the tall red-haired girl currently trying not to look sheepish in front of her. Margaret was definitely disturbed by the fact she found a student attractive, as she never had before. And Rory definitely went against type for her, at least outwardly.

She had only had a scattering of relationships in her lifetime, and even fewer casual encounters such as the one in Denver, but all of those women had had something in common: they were all stuffy academic types, just as she knew herself to be. Margaret knew she was something of an anomaly in the theater department; most people in her field were loud and boisterous and definitely not ones to shy away from their emotions. She was none of those things. She was a bookish nerd from way back. She knew and accepted this about herself. It didn't bother her, as she was her father's daughter through and through. What drew her to theater was the pure art of it, the being able to create something and have it speak to a whole roomful of people and receive the immediate feedback from them, that they appreciated what was done and that it spoke to them. Though writing was something she also enjoyed, and she was currently working on a book, it lacked that instant connection with the audience.

Rory seemed more like the theater people she was used to, though she didn't know her very well. There was a spark there and a seeming ease with others that Margaret always wished she had. During rehearsals, the girl laughed and joked with the other cast members as if they were all old friends, even if they had just met. During downtime, Rory could often be seen sitting in some far-off corner of the stage, leaning back on her hands or against the wall, with her legs out in front of her, smiling and chatting. And she did have a nice smile, Margaret had to admit. It really did light up her whole face, as clichéd as that sounded.

As she was lecturing, Margaret swept her gaze across the room, and as her eyes fell on Rory again, the girl gave her a small smile. It was faint but lovely and it made Margaret stumble over her words.

"So, what Shakespeare was getting at...was...um...sorry, brain freeze." She had to quickly look away as the class giggled. Recovering, she started over. "Shakespeare dealt with the multitude of human emotions and motivators, and that's why one could use his work to study human psychology, which many have done. Love, greed, and jealousy were his main themes." As Margaret got herself back on track, she resumed her usual pacing in the front of the room, making sure not to make extended eye contact with Rory again.

❖

Rehearsals had moved into an actual theater space once the play was cast, and on Friday, Rory was sitting in the front row of seats, as they weren't currently working on a scene with her in it. If she wasn't backstage during downtime, she was sitting in the front row so her legs could be stretched out in front of her, as scrunching them up in any of the other rows was always uncomfortable. There just never seemed to be enough space in theaters for tall people.

She was watching Dr. Parks, who was standing in the

middle of the center aisle, directing the scene. She looked so small, but no less fierce or attractive for all that. Dr. Parks had one hand on her hip and the other was holding a clipboard, on which Rory had often seen her take notes, which she would share with the cast. During rehearsal, Dr. Parks's sleeves would be rolled up, her hair would start to come unwound from its braid, and her glasses would often spend the entire time pushed up on her head. She looked tired, which wasn't surprising, since it was now almost eight on Friday night, and Rory guessed she had been going strong all day. She wondered when they would be let out of rehearsal, not because she was anxious to go, but because she suddenly felt protective of Dr. Parks, though she wasn't sure why.

"What are you staring at?" Suddenly, Miranda was sitting next to her and demanding her attention.

Reluctantly, Rory turned and faced her. "Nothing, just watching rehearsal."

There was an unmistakable smirk on Miranda's face. "Looks to me like you were watching something else."

Rory narrowed her eyes. She knew Miranda was not someone with whom she could suddenly start gushing about her crush, not that she was the type to do much of that anyway. "What are you talking about?"

"Come on, I saw you staring at Dr. Parks. I mean, she's not as hot as Dr. Baskin, who's nothing but smoky sex, but I suppose she's cute." Miranda winked, like they shared a secret.

Rory gave her a fake smile. "You're right about Dr. Baskin. I was totally surprised to find out she was dating Dr. Duncan. I mean, he's a guy—I thought for sure she was family." Rory hoped her attempt at diversion worked.

"God, I know, and I heard he totally cheated on his wife, and then left her for Dr. Baskin."

"I hadn't heard that."

"Oh, yeah. Happened like five years ago. Apparently it was a major scandal. His wife used to teach in our department but she left when it all happened."

"I don't blame her." As Miranda continued to gossip, Rory was glad her attention had been diverted. She was sad that she couldn't turn around and watch Dr. Parks, though, while Miranda was sitting next to her and watching her every move. So she pretended to be interested in Miranda's story and tried not to flinch each time Miranda put her hand on Rory's arm anytime she wanted to emphasize a point.

When her story was over, Miranda looked almost shyly at Rory. "So, I was wondering if you wanted to get together after rehearsal. Maybe get a bite to eat?"

Somewhat surprised, Rory asked, "Are you asking me out?"

"Trying to, yeah." Miranda giggled.

"Oh."

"Oh? What kind of answer is that?"

Even without her crush on Dr. Parks, Rory knew she wouldn't want to go out with Miranda. "I'm sorry. I can't." Rory felt like an ass. You would think she would be good at turning people down, since getting asked out by people she didn't want to go out with was not new to her.

"You can't? Are you seeing someone or something?"

"No, it's just that…the truth is, you seem like a nice person but you're not my type. I'm sorry." Phew, she did it.

"You don't even know me, how can you say that? We might have more in common than you think."

"Maybe. I'm just attracted to a particular kind of girl, that's all." That much was true.

"What, like Dr. Parks?"

"No, that's not what I meant."

"Whatever. Good luck with that." Miranda stood up

abruptly and stalked off. Inwardly, Rory breathed easier and was glad she could go back to fantasizing about her professor.

❖

When Margaret finally called an end to rehearsal, it was approaching nine, and she hoped she didn't look as tired as she felt. She sighed and stretched her back.

"Dr. Parks?"

Margaret turned to Rory with a tired smile. "Yes, Rory?"

"You look beat. Let me get you some dinner." She smiled and tried to act as if she hadn't just kinda-sorta asked out her teacher.

Margaret chuckled and shook her head. "Oh no, you don't need to babysit me. You go and have fun. It's Friday night, enjoy it."

Suddenly sounding shy, Rory said, "No, I wasn't thinking of it as babysitting you. I just thought it would be fun, is all."

"If your idea of fun means spending Friday night with your professor, then you're in trouble."

"Remember, I'm a grad student—I don't have time for a social life."

"Maybe you should change that. But I'm no one to talk. I can't remember when I last had one either."

"See, we're equally pathetic in that way. What do you say to a nice cheeseburger? I know a place." Rory smiled.

"Okay, I'll let you take me away from all this. Do you have a car?"

"No, I take the bus or I walk."

"All right, I'll drive. Follow me."

To say Margaret was surprised by the invitation would have been an understatement. She wasn't sure if she had actually been asked out or if the girl just felt sorry for the state she was in and had had a sudden urge to take care of her. Either way, it caught her off guard. Then she realized that she was probably overthinking things, and Rory was just inviting her out of genuine concern. It wasn't unusual for grad students and professors to hang out or share a meal. That was normal. Margaret kicked herself for her immediate response and decided that it was only a cheeseburger. And she had to admit that she was hungry. And all she had waiting for her at home was an article she had been dragging her feet on finishing.

The place Rory picked was a hole-in-the-wall, not usually frequented by college students as there was nothing trendy about it. The floor was scuffed and worn and the vinyl was peeling off the booths. But the food was great and it was cheap.

"How'd you find this place?" Margaret took it all in in wonder. It wasn't the kind of diner she would normally be drawn to, as she preferred more refined places. But, though worn, the place definitely held an old-fashioned appeal.

"I was out for a walk one day and came across it. It's cool, isn't it?" Rory grinned and Margaret laughed at her enthusiasm.

"It definitely reminds me of an old fifties diner."

"You make it sound as if you were there, but this era was way before your time too."

"That's true. Sometimes it doesn't feel that way though."

"Probably because of that no-social-life thing we talked about earlier." Rory took a bite of a French fry and nodded knowingly.

"And when was the last time you had one, Miss Grad Student?"

"Probably last year sometime."

"Well, it's been longer for me."

"See, we both needed this. I think my real job, in addition to being Maggie, will be to make sure you have some fun."

"Fun? Who says my life is lacking fun? Just because I only go from home to work and back again, doesn't mean—" Margaret was cut off by a projectile straw wrapper that hit one of her lenses before falling in the pool of ketchup on her plate. She looked down at it, then up at Rory, who was trying to conceal her laughter and failing. Trying to sound menacing, Margaret said, "I can still fail you, you know? That was uncalled for." She gingerly picked the wrapper out of her ketchup.

Rory stopped laughing. "I'm sorry, Dr. Parks. Just trying to lighten the mood a lit—" A French fry sailed across the table and landed in her curls. She looked down at the offending fry, then up at Margaret, who was actually giggling. She delicately took the fry out of her hair and placed it on the table. "This is going to be an interesting semester."

Margaret laughed out loud at Rory's calmness. It'd been a while since she'd had reason to, and it felt good. She liked this young woman and was glad she would be working with her. Maybe Rory could help her relax, Margaret thought, not completely sure what she meant by that.

Chapter Four

They were three weeks into rehearsal, and their Friday night cheeseburger had become routine. They always started talking about that day's rehearsal, then moved on to other topics. Rory was glad to see that she could make Margaret—about a week ago, she'd invited the cast to drop her formal title outside of class—laugh.

"So, initial teasing aside, are you having fun? Have you gotten a social life yet?" Margaret nonchalantly ate her burger as she asked this question, as if it wasn't that big of a deal.

Rory swallowed the bite she had in her mouth before it was fully chewed and coughed at the effort. Margaret laughed and Rory narrowed her eyes at her. "What, this doesn't count?"

"I meant with people your own age."

"Oh, just Rachel sometimes, when she's not too busy. But other than that, you're my social life." Rory smiled sheepishly at her and shrugged.

"Rachel?"

"A floor mate and a sister-from-another-mister. She'd like to be more but I just don't see her that way. She's cute and fun and we have a good time together, but sometimes she's a little too much fun, if you know what I mean." Rory wasn't sure, but she thought she had heard a note of something other than polite interest in Margaret's question. But she told herself not to read too much into it. The professor was probably just genuinely curious.

"I see. So if Rachel isn't the right girl for you, who would be?"

Rory was definitely glad she wasn't eating when Margaret had asked that question. She almost said, *Someone like you*, but checked herself. Instead, she said, "Someone who is mature enough to hold an intelligent conversation, who takes life and the world seriously, but who also knows how to get silly and goofy at the same time. Someone who knows who she is, for the most part, and where she's going." Rory grinned. "And someone who is much shorter than me."

Margaret laughed. "Glad you don't give us vertically challenged people short shrift."

Rory laughed out loud. Feeling bold, she asked, "What about you, Margaret? Who would be your ideal?" They had never discussed Margaret's personal life before, so Rory still didn't know if she was gay.

"Well, hmm. I agree with everything you said, though there is no height requirement to ride this ride." She said it deadpan and Rory nearly did a spit take.

"Oh my God." Rory was laughing and coughing at the same time. "Did you just…?"

Margaret was laughing at Rory's reaction. "Oh yes, I did. Problem?"

Rory grabbed a napkin and wiped her mouth. "Oh, Professor, you are full of surprises."

"Well, before I was your professor, I did indeed have a social life, though it has been quite a while." Margaret hesitated. Rory waited patiently, giving Margaret the space she needed. "The women I've dated, not that there have been that many, have all been a lot like me—boring academics whose idea of fun was a rousing game of gin rummy if there wasn't an art opening or conference to go to." Margaret offered a sheepish smile and a shrug.

"Well, first off, you're not boring, and second of all, if you found them boring, why did you date them?"

"See, it makes so much sense when you put it that way."

Rory said, "Dating should make sense, though it seldom does."

"Indeed. Have you had much luck with dating?"

"Truth?"

Margaret nodded.

"Not much, but it's hard when you want someone who doesn't act like a giggling imbecile."

Margaret laughed. "I assume you're talking about girls your own age." At Rory's nod, she continued, "Don't you think you're being too hard on them?"

Rory sighed. "Maybe, but I do want someone on the more serious side. I also want someone who believes in romance, not sex in the moment. I want to woo someone and, dammit, no one wants to be wooed."

"There are plenty of women who want that. Maybe you just need to surround yourself with a different group of lesbians. I'm sure they're on campus somewhere."

Rory wasn't smiling when she locked eyes with Margaret and said, "I think you're right." Rory held her gaze for a moment, neither one of them saying anything. Then Margaret broke the hold first.

Almost whispering, Margaret said, "You shouldn't look at me like that. I'm your teacher."

Keeping her own voice low, Rory said, "Not my teacher, my *professor*, my grad-school professor—and I'm old enough to know what I want."

"Rory...I think this conversation has gone somewhere it

shouldn't and I take responsibility for that. Maybe we should go." Margaret started to leave. Rory put her hand on Margaret's hand to stop her.

Margaret looked at their clasped hands. Rory was lightly brushing her thumb over Margaret's fingers. She closed her eyes and squeezed Rory's hand, then let go and put her hand in her lap. But she locked eyes with Rory and gave her a small smile. "Rory, I'm forty years old."

"So?"

"I'm your professor."

"Easily remedied." Rory smiled, enjoying this game. She knew she could bat away any objection Margaret could throw.

"I don't really discuss my private life at work."

"Then we won't tell them."

Margaret smiled. "What would your parents say?"

"They're happy when I'm happy."

"What makes you so sure I'd make you happy?"

"Blind faith."

"I'm not so sure I have any of that."

"Margaret, can I ask you a question?"

"Yes."

"What are you really afraid of?"

"Maybe just—you're so young, you haven't experienced much yet, and you want me." She shook her head. "I won't say I'm flattered because that expression is overused and often makes the person feel worse. But, really, what could I possibly offer that girls your own age couldn't?"

"Oh, Margaret…why not you? You're beautiful, passionate about what you do, you're funny and fierce. You're a total badass. I don't even have to say brilliant, it's there in your honorific."

"I'm not sure I agree with your assessment. You make me sound way better than I am. That being said, I've never been called a badass before—now that is flattering. But you could say most of that about girls your own age."

Realizing she was going to have to get in closer to the heart of the matter, Rory tried again. "Most girls my age are silly and act dumb even when they're not. And the serious ones, the ones who rally for causes and organize events, get offended by the slightest things. They take themselves too seriously. I should be able to call myself a dyke if I want to, which I do on occasion, without some little lesbian hipster with a short haircut and an expensive coffee addiction saying it offends her." Margaret laughed. "You're not like that. You already know who you are, so you don't have to fake it or try too hard."

Still chuckling, Margaret said, "Be fair. It takes a while to be settled in your identity. They're still figuring themselves out."

"Are you completely figured out?"

"Well, no, but…"

"See, but you hide it better. I don't want to date a kid, and that's what they are to me."

Margaret asked playfully, "Then why me and not any of your other professors?"

Realizing she was being baited, Rory replied, "Good point. I wonder what Dr. Baskin is doing right now." She moved as if to leave.

"Don't you dare!" Margaret instantly reached out and grabbed Rory's arm.

Rory looked down at the hand holding her and back up at Margaret and said softly, "So you do care."

It was Margaret's turn to caress Rory this time, and as she did so, Rory sat back in her seat. Margaret didn't say anything for a moment, just held Rory's gaze. "So much so that I think I need to take you to your dorm before I do something foolish."

Rory grinned. "All right, Doc, have it your way. You can take me home."

"That's not what I meant and you know it, smart-ass. And you know how I feel about being called *Doc*. I won't let Davis call me that, and I've known him longer. What makes you think you can, hmm?" Margaret gave a flippant grin as she got up from the booth.

Rory leaned in and whispered, "Yeah, but you know me better." Rory topped her quip off with a wink.

Margaret shook her head. "Just get in the car or I'll leave your ass here."

They were laughing together as they left but Rory glimpsed Miranda, sitting at a corner table with a friend. Miranda caught Rory's eye and made a show of looking from Margaret and back to Rory, then smirked at them.

Margaret knew she needed a nice glass of wine and some good company. After she dropped Rory back on campus, she called Bill to invite herself over. He and Dix were home having a movie night.

"If you're having couples time, I don't want to intrude."

"Not really, just two old men sitting on the couch, pretending not to cry at *Beaches*."

Margaret laughed. "I'm not sure I want to get in the middle of that."

"Oh, please, how many times can you watch Barbara Hershey die?"

Margaret heard Dix in the background saying, "Apparently, thirty-six."

Bill said, "Hush," to his husband, then to Margaret, "I

hear something funny in your voice. Get your skinny butt over here and we can talk about what ails you."

Margaret gave a sigh of relief. She loved that Bill always knew when she needed a friend to talk to and never shied away from being that friend for her. "Well, if you're sure. There is a little something personal I need to discuss."

"Something about your personal life?"

"Sort of."

"Did you finally get one?"

"No, but not for someone's lack of trying."

"Someone is pursuing you? Ooh, congrats. Now hang up and get over here so you can tell me everything."

Margaret couldn't help but laugh. "You are such a vicious gossip."

There was laugher in Bill's voice when he asked, "Are you stereotyping me?"

"I would never. I'll be there in five." She drove to Bill and Dix's place with a smile on her face, already feeling somewhat better and thinking that she might have overreacted at the diner.

Five minutes later, before she could knock on the door, it was opened by Bill, who put a glass of wine in her hand before she could say more than, "Hello."

"Here, drink this, it makes everything feel better."

Margaret did as told. "Mm. Thank you. You are a true friend. Just what I needed." She stepped all the way in and Bill closed the door behind her.

Dix came in from the kitchen with his own drink and kissed her on the cheek. "Hello, good-looking. I hear you have a story to tell."

"It's no big deal, really."

"Let us be the judge of that. Come on." Dix grabbed her hand and led her over to the sofa, and Bill followed. She ended up sitting between them. "So, tell Uncle Dix about this pursuer and why you're not overjoyed about it. Is it a man?" Dix had a look of mock horror on his face.

Margaret laughed and pulled one leg up underneath herself. "No, I almost wish it were though. At least then I would know what to do about it."

"So, it's a woman. That's progress."

"Yes, but it's the wrong woman. Well, girl, actually."

"Oh, honey…please tell me you're not talking about that Lolita from your classroom."

"What Lolita from your classroom? Have you committed the unoriginal sin of sleeping with a student?" Dix looked horrified and amused at the same time.

"No." She turned to Bill. "You didn't tell him?"

"He doesn't tell me everything. So start over…Who are we talking about?"

Margaret sighed. "Okay, there's this very attractive red-haired grad student in one of my classes. All I've done is notice that she's attractive. Well, she's also been cast in my play this semester, which means I see her all the time, it seems like. After the first week of rehearsal, she asked me if I wanted to go out for a bite to eat."

"Wait, she asked you out? Please tell me you didn't say yes."

"Bill, it was only a burger. There was nothing wrong with getting a bite to eat."

"It's never just a burger or just coffee. There's always subtext."

Margaret smiled over her glass of wine. "So, is this not just wine?"

Dix leaned into her in a playful way and put his hand around hers that was holding the wineglass. "Oh, honey, it's

always more than just wine. I want your...mind...so much."
He winked, then kissed her on the cheek. She giggled.

"Don't mind him," Bill said. "He's such a big flirt. So, did
you bite off more than you can chew?"

Margaret turned her attention back to Bill. "Not on
purpose. We've been going to get a burger every Friday for
the past three weeks. Just talking, mostly about the play, her
other classes, life in general. I thought we might even work
our way to becoming friends. She's really mature for her age."
Both Bill and Dix rolled their eyes. "What?"

"That's what they all say," Bill drawled.

"First the Lolita reference, now this. You're starting to
make me feel like a pedophile, and I didn't do anything. Plus,
she's way over the age of consent." She wasn't mad at them,
but they were touching on things she had been trying to ignore.

"I'm sorry, love, we didn't mean to. Go on."

"Sorry, it's just that after tonight, I'm feeling a bit as if I
did do something wrong and I wish I could shake the feeling."
She proceeded to tell them about the hand-holding and Rory's
confession that Margaret was her type, and mentioned that
Miranda had seen the whole thing.

"That's all you need is some little Amy Fisher trying to
start trouble." Dix shook his head as he was refilling her wine.

Bill rolled his eyes. "Look at you with the nineties pop-
culture reference that no one remembers anymore. But he's
right. My question is, who does this Miranda have it in for
more, you or the little red-headed girl?"

"She's not so little—she's almost a foot taller than I am.
And I'm not sure, though I think she's got a crush on my
student. She often flirts obviously with her during rehearsals."

"So she has a crush on your red-haired Supergirl and has
now seen something that could easily be misinterpreted..."

"And she wouldn't be misinterpreting." Margaret sighed.

"And you're afraid that she'll do something sinister with this information. Did I get all the bullet points?"

"Very succulently, yes. The question is, where do I go from here?"

"Where do you want to go?"

Margaret cocked an eyebrow at Dix. "What do you mean?"

"Just what do you want, Margaret Parks? What would make you happy?" The men shared a smile.

"You're asking me if I really want to go out with her, aren't you."

"Do you?"

Margaret didn't say anything for a long moment, just stared out in front of her into empty air. After a moment, she said, "Sometimes I do. But I know better."

"Oh, honey." Dix put his hand on her shoulder.

"I know."

"What are you so sad for? So she's your student—big deal! It's not as if this never happens. All the better when it's consensual between two people who might actually care for each other, and not when one is just trying to get something from the other one." Bill was ever the romantic.

"Honey, you know it's more than that." Dix was having none of it. "Can you imagine the headline? *Lesbian professor caught sleeping with her student. Board investigates.* It would be a shit storm, and you know as well as I do that the board hates a queer shit storm."

"That's what I'm afraid of." Margaret was relieved they understood. "So I've decided to stop with the after-rehearsal burgers and just keep things on a professional level. It's the right thing to do." Margaret rose from the couch and took her glass into the kitchen. When she came back, she said, "Thank you, boys. You always know the right thing to say. Now, I should go."

Bill walked her to the door. "Are you sure you're safe to drive?"

"Bill, I love your concern, but don't forget, I'm an Irish girl from Boston. One glass of wine is nothing." She kissed him on the cheek. "Good night, my friend." She waved to Dix.

Bill leaned in and said in a serious tone, "Margaret, don't let some little vengeful coed scare you away from what could be a real shot at happiness. If you want this girl and she wants you, give it a shot. You never know what might happen. Sometimes, finding out the answer to what-if can be a beautiful and powerful thing. Just promise me you'll think about it."

"I'll give it some thought. Good night."

Chapter Five

The next Friday, after Margaret called it quits and everyone headed out of the theater on their way to whatever plans they had next, Rory quickly gathered her things and hurried up to Margaret, who was already walking out the door. She hadn't said anything to Rory, which was unusual. Margaret hadn't said a personal word to her all week in class, even seemed to be avoiding eye contact. So Rory had slumped in her seat, taking notes, acting as bored as the rest of her classmates, but really, she was perplexed.

She was by Margaret's side in three strides. "Hey, hold on."

Margaret stopped. She turned in Rory's direction and gave her a small smile. "Oh, Rory, I'm sorry, I should have told you earlier, I won't be able to get a burger with you tonight. I have a ton of work to do at home and I'm going to be holed up all weekend when I'm not here. Sorry, that's where my mind has been."

"With all due respect, I call bullshit." They were friends, weren't they? She gave Margaret a smile to show that she wasn't upset or trying to get snippy. "Margaret, you've been avoiding me all week. I've noticed. You don't have to go out with me tonight but I'd just like you to tell me what's going on." She lowered her already low voice to a near whisper. "Look, I'm sorry it got a little weird and tense last week. I didn't mean to make you feel pressured. The truth is, I really like you, and I really enjoy hanging out with you."

Margaret sighed and looked down for a moment, then looked Rory in the eyes. "I greatly enjoy your company as well but I don't think hanging out that way would be appropriate. People may get the wrong idea."

Rory's back tensed and she said icily, "You mean people like Miranda?"

"Exactly. Rory, I'm sure you're aware of the stigma a professor carries when they're accused of an inappropriate relationship with a student—even a grad student. The professor doesn't have to do anything wrong—often, the accusation is enough. Look, this isn't the time or place for this discussion, but I just think, for the time being, we should confine our interactions to what happens in the theater and the classroom. Maybe when you're not in my classroom anymore, we can revisit the idea of being friends." Margaret shrugged. "That is, if you'd still want to."

Rory was sure she'd visibly deflated. She understood everything Margaret said but understanding didn't bring comfort. "I get it. I don't want to make things hard for you." She took a step back and said in a more normal tone, "I'll see you tomorrow, Dr. Parks."

Margaret gave Rory a tired, sad smile. "Good-bye, Rory." Then she left.

Rory stood in the aisle, looking wistfully at the now-closed door, and sighed. She was just about to leave when she heard someone walking behind her and groaned when she saw that it was Miranda with a smirk on her face. She was not in the mood for this. "What's your problem?"

"Me? I don't have a problem. Looks like you do, though. What happened? I thought things were going well with you and Mrs. Robinson." There was an evil twinkle in her eyes that made Rory realize just how much Miranda seemed to thrive on the misery of others.

Several retorts came to mind, but she bit them all back. It just wasn't worth it. Ignoring Miranda, Rory turned back around and walked toward the door. Before she was out, she heard Miranda softly singing the nonsense bits of the Simon & Garfunkel song loud enough so she could hear, then laughing to herself about it. Rory quickened her pace down the hallway, slammed through the front double doors of Maguire Hall, and was outside, striding back to her dorm. It wasn't the fact that Margaret didn't want to date her that got to her, it was that she was afraid to even be friends. Why should they let assholes like Miranda dictate their lives? Rory angrily kicked a pile of leaves that had blown across the sidewalk and muttered, "Fuck it." She pulled out her cell and texted Rachel.

Unless you're getting laid tonight, you're getting me drunk.

Then will I be getting laid?

Rory smiled. Rachel never changed and she was glad for it.

I can't predict who you'll do, except it won't be me. Just take me away from all this.

Okay. I'll meet you at my car.

After Margaret had left Bill and Dix's place the week before, she had spent a lot of time thinking over the weekend. She really did enjoy getting to know Rory, and their time spent together was always filled with laughter, something Margaret realized had been missing from her life for quite some time. Other than the time she spent with Bill and Dix, of course. But the more she thought about it, she realized how dangerous their friendship could be. Rory just had a crush on her; she'd get over it. And even if Rory thought the feelings were very real, she was sure they were transitory.

As for herself, she wasn't sure what to think. She knew she felt a strong attraction to Rory that went beyond physical. And as stupid as it would sound out loud, she really did like the girl's mind. They seemed to be…connected, on the same wavelength, and that's the part that scared her the most. She came to the conclusion that she had to put a stop to their hanging out, because it would only complicate their lives.

Rory had looked so crestfallen when Margaret had canceled their post-rehearsal plans and called time on their personal relationship that she had to fight the urge to relent. She'd thought if she listened close enough, she could hear Rory's heart breaking.

Hearing Rory going back to calling her by her formal title hurt, but she couldn't help but think that in the long run, it was for the best. She'd left the theater and forced herself not to look back.

As promised, Rachel was waiting next to her car by the time Rory made it to the parking lot. She was leaning against her door with her arms crossed over her chest, looking as if she had all the time in the world. That Rachel was attractive, there was no question. She filled out her jeans and sweater quite nicely, and the suede boots she was currently wearing lent her a few more inches. As usual, her long blond hair was free-flowing and natural. Rory appreciated her in many ways, just not in *that* way.

Rachel looked Rory up and down. "You look like hell. Just how bad was rehearsal?"

Rory felt examined and wasn't sure how to feel about that. "It was hell, thank you for noticing." Instead of getting in the car, Rory stood next to Rachel and rested her head on Rachel's shoulder. She sighed.

Rachel kissed the top of Rory's head, then leaned her own against Rory's. "You going to tell me what's really wrong?"

"Not right now. Maybe after you get me drunk."

"So are you saying I can have my wicked way with you then?"

Rory stood up straight and gave Rachel a small smile. "I don't know about that, but you might get me to talk."

"Talking? That's boring. But if it's what you want to do, I'll listen. Now, get in the car."

They made their way to one of the local bars that catered to college students. It played club music and served drinks in yard-long glasses and shots in test-tube-shaped glasses. Rory hated it, Rachel loved it.

Before they went inside, Rory asked, "Why did you bring me here, of all places?"

Rachel put her arm around Rory's waist. "Because it's private."

"Rachel, there's a few hundred college students in there. How is this private?"

"Because, dear heart, you can tell me all your troubles and no one will be able to hear you."

"Why does that sound like you're saying that no one can hear me scream?" In response, Rachel just gave her an evil grin.

The constant thumping became louder the closer they got to the door. House music always made Rory's ears hurt and all the songs sounded to her like one long-drawn-out series of percussion beats, with strobe lights thrown in for that extra seizure-inducing flair. This bar would definitely not have been

Rory's first choice to get her drunk on, but she had put her woes in Rachel's hands and she had to trust her friend. She good-naturedly put her arm around Rachel's shoulders as they walked up to the door.

After they each got a beer at the bar, Rachel took Rory by the hand and led her to a corner table with high stools. Once they were seated, she clinked her bottle to Rory's and leaned in to say, "Cheers, my friend."

"Salud!" Rory didn't actually speak Spanish, but thanks to Rachel, she could now toast in five languages besides English. Despite the thumping music, she tried to relax into the general mood of the place and enjoy that she was there with her best friend and just appreciate the moment. She really had no reason to feel so down and out of sorts. It's not as if she and Margaret had broken up or anything. They had shared a few dinners and some conversation, nothing more.

After they had both downed about half their bottles, Rachel said, "So, what's up?"

Rory sighed. "Not much. I think I just built something up in my head and broke my own heart when it didn't happen the way I hoped it would."

Rachel cocked an eyebrow. "Really? Are you saying that my little Aurora just got her heart broken?"

"In a matter of speaking."

Rachel pounded her fist on the table in mock righteous indignation. "Who's this bitch who broke your heart? Bring me her head!"

Rory laughed. "She didn't really do anything. Like I said, I let myself think that something was going to happen with her, but it didn't. I have only myself to blame."

"Oh, Morgan, what have I told you about falling for unobtainable girls?"

"I know. Couldn't help myself."

"I know you want to find someone special, you deserve to, but next time, try to make sure she's available."

"Technically, she is, just not to me, apparently."

"Well, if the universe thinks you should be together, then you will. In the meantime, have another beer."

"I think I read that on a poster in your room."

"You did. Right next to the one that says shut up and dance." With that, Rachel yanked Rory out of her chair and onto the dance floor. Rory had no idea how to dance to house, but she copied Rachel and just concentrated on not looking like an ass. Before she knew it, she was covered in glitter and had a good buzz on, her problems from earlier all but forgotten.

❖

Saturday morning, Rory rolled out of bed with a spinning head, a dead cat in her mouth, and waves in her stomach. "Fuck you, Rachel," she muttered. She knew it wasn't her friend's fault that she got wasted the night before. It was all on her. She didn't have to keep drinking the little tube drinks or half a brewery. Part of the problem was that she wasn't much of a drinker, so she hadn't built up the same tolerance Rachel had. She should have quit way sooner than she did but she chose not to. She fell back on her bed with a groan, holding her stomach. She was grateful there was no one else in her bed. At least she hadn't been completely stupid. She vaguely remembered someone flirting with her, although she couldn't focus on who it had been. She just remembered Rachel pretending to be her date and the person backing off. She wasn't sure why that was the one thing she remembered from the evening. She ran a hand over her face, thinking she would just stay in bed until the nausea passed. Whatever she had to do today could wait, she reasoned.

Then with a start, she remembered: rehearsal. She glanced at the digital clock on the shelf above her desk. She had originally placed it there instead of next to her bed with the thought that if she had to get out of bed to turn off the alarm, she might as well stay up. It didn't always work. Some mornings she had no problem crawling back into bed and sleeping for another hour or two, depending on what she had to do that day. She squinted in the brightness: 10:45. Shit. How the hell was she going to make it to Maguire Hall, a distance that took about ten minutes to walk sober, in fifteen minutes, when she couldn't even stand up yet, let alone get dressed and walk across campus?

"I can do this," she muttered. She put one foot on the floor, then slowly the other one, and then sat up more slowly still. When she opened her eyes she realized she was still in her clothes from the night before. Well, that would save her some time. She gingerly rose from the bed and stood in one spot for a moment, trying to figure out if her stomach was going to turn on her. It seemed okay. She grabbed her toothbrush off her dresser and was on her way out the door to go to the communal bathroom, when she caught a glimpse of herself in the square mirror on the wall next to the closet. Her curls were a massive unruly mess. They were sticking up every which way. Figuring there was no getting a brush through it until after a shower and knowing she didn't have time for one, she resigned herself to it being a hat day.

Rory brushed her teeth, put a hat on, grabbed her keys, and went. Thankfully, she was able to make the walk without her stomach turning on her, but the sun was still way too bright. She wished she had remembered her sunglasses, though the hat helped some. When she got to the theater, she was lucky enough to be only ten minutes late but still felt badly about it, considering she was one of the leads. Luckily, they hadn't started yet, which wasn't unusual, as time seemed to have little meaning during rehearsals. The crew was still arranging the furniture on the set and the cast members were reading their scripts. Margaret was in her usual seat in the front row, sitting next to an underclassmen she had hired earlier in the week to be her stage manager. They had their heads bent, conferring.

Rory was trying to act as if nothing was wrong as she casually made her way to a seat in the front row on the opposite side of the aisle from Margaret. Only when she sat down did she realize that she had forgotten her script. Margaret finished talking to the stage manager and turned in Rory's direction. Apparently her late entrance had not gone unnoticed.

"Rory, glad you could make it."

"Sorry, Mar…Dr. Parks." She slunk down in her seat.

Margaret walked over to her and stood next to her seat. Rory immediately sat up. Margaret cocked her head. "You're sparkly and smell like a brewery. This doesn't seem like you."

Rory shrugged, feeling defiant. "Sometimes it is, I guess. I am a student, after all." Margaret looked as if she had been struck. Rory hadn't meant for her words to come out as harshly as they did or to sting as badly as they appeared to, and she immediately regretted it but felt trying to take it back would only make things worse.

"Yes, you are. Sometimes I forget that. I don't care what you do on your off time, but try to make it to rehearsal on time, and preferably take a shower first."

"Sorry." There was nothing else she could say to that.

Margaret said nothing more to her and walked away, then she called out, "All right, I need Brick and Big Daddy." Davis and Steven, the actor playing Big Daddy, took their positions onstage. They began to play a scene, and the more the lines referred to self-pity, the more Rory sank into her seat again, feeling sorry for herself. The words hit too close to home. At one point, Margaret turned to her and raised an eyebrow, and gave her a pointed look.

Margaret called for a scene between Maggie and Brick next. As Rory took the stage, she was grateful that she had a good memory and had already memorized the script, so she'd have no problem remembering her lines.

But before they could begin the scene, Margaret addressed her. "Rory, I know this is not a dress rehearsal, but could you take the hat off, please? It's too distracting to see Maggie in a Cubs cap." Everyone snickered.

"I don't think you want me to do that." Rory knew her hair, now flattened by the hat, would be in even worse shape than it had been when she had woken up that morning.

"Yes, I think I do. Bad hair day notwithstanding, take it off, please."

"Okay, you asked for it." She took the hat off and threw it offstage, toward the seat she had been sitting in. It landed a few feet from it. As expected, her hair was flat in some places and oddly askew in others.

"Oh, honey." Davis tsked in sympathy. Everyone else chuckled. Rory shrugged it off.

"All right, fun's over, back to work. Continue, please."

Rory and Davis continued the scene. Rory was thankful that her stomach seemed to be getting better and normalcy was returning.

When they finished rehearsal, Margaret called to Rory before she could get out the door. "Rory, can I see you a moment?"

Somewhat surprised, Rory picked up her hat from the aisle and walked over to Margaret's chair. The stage manager was nowhere in sight. Rory thought she knew what was coming. "I'm sorry for being late. It won't happen again."

"Rory, are you all right?" Margaret spoke more softly this

time, not as she had the last time. Gone was the stern professor-director; now she spoke as a friend. "I only ask because getting wasted doesn't seem to be your norm. I can't help feeling that I might somehow be responsible for that."

"That's stupid, you didn't get me drunk. I did."

"I mean...I thought maybe our conversation yesterday might have had something to do with it."

"Don't worry about it. I take responsibility for my own actions. I may be young, but I know how to admit my mistakes." Rory wasn't sure why she was saying such cruel things, but she couldn't seem to stop herself.

"I see." Margaret adopted the pose of stern professor again. "Just try not to make a habit of it, hmm? I'll see you in class." Margaret turned away to gather up her things, effectively dismissing Rory.

Rory stood there for a moment, too stunned to move. Then she gathered herself and said, "Right. See ya Monday, Dr. Parks." Then she turned and left, not looking back.

❖

Margaret couldn't believe it when she had seen Rory walking in, obviously hungover. It seemed so out of character for her, not that Margaret knew her well enough to judge. Rory had just seemed too mature to spend her time drinking to excess. She'd taken in Rory's slept-in clothes, her curls sticking out from underneath the hat, the glitter—glitter!—that caught the light, to say nothing of the smell that wafted across the aisle to her. She couldn't help but feel responsible, even though Rory was an adult who could make her own decisions.

She really did want to try to be friends with Rory; she just knew that right now was not the best time. The fact that grad students and professors were often friends who hung out together off campus wasn't the point. It was that as a lesbian, her actions were more scrutinized than her straight colleagues', even though you might expect a theater department to be a liberal place. After all, her department did seem to be the best department on campus to be queer. But to the campus at large, gay professors were still looked upon as an anomaly and expected to mind their p's and q's; and most of them did. The unspoken rule was that you could be out on campus, even bring your significant other to events, just don't make a spectacle about it. A spectacle was usually defined as being undignified; the queer community had a different term for the expected behavior: straight-acting. Hanging out with a female student, an openly gay one at that and one who was technically *her* student, would draw attention, especially when there were people like Miranda around to made an issue of it.

Still, Margaret felt guilty for any hurt she might have caused Rory. When was she going to figure out the whole communicating-with-women thing? Something Bill once said came back to her: *Women are insane and confusing, how can you date them?*

Apparently, she liked a challenge. And Rory was turning out to be more challenging than any woman she had ever dated before, and they weren't even dating.

Just as she was about to leave, Miranda walked up to her with a smile on her face. "Dr. Parks, is everything all right?"

Startled by the question, Margaret answered, "Yes. Why do you ask?"

"Well, I just saw Rory leave in a huff, the same as last week. And it was hard to miss the state she was in when she came in." Miranda took on a conspirator's tone, as if she and Margaret were sharing a secret.

Margaret took in the look on Miranda's face and the tone in her voice and could tell how much she was enjoying the whole situation. Miranda was a mean girl, and Margaret was not going to play her game. "I didn't notice any huff, and as for Rory's state, that's none of my concern, nor should it be yours. Now, I have to go." Margaret started to walk away but Miranda kept pace with her.

"Well, I was just thinking that if she's going to be a constant bother like this, then you might want to consider recasting her part."

Margaret stopped in her tracks and faced Miranda. "Is that what this is about?"

Miranda asked innocently, "What what's about?"

Suddenly incensed, Margaret took on an even harsher tone with Miranda then she had with Rory. "Miranda, the play is cast, and that's final. If you're unhappy with your part, I have a whole list of other young women who would gladly take it instead. And if you're trying to imply anything else, what Rory does on her own time is none of your business."

"I have no idea what you mean. I'm happy with my part, I was just trying to—"

"You were trying to get involved in something that is none of your business. Please confine your interests to the play at hand, hmm?"

"That's what I was trying to do. I only want what's best for the show. I didn't want you humiliated with having a boozer for a lead."

"Rory is not..." Margaret stopped herself, realizing how defensive she was getting, and cursed herself for letting the girl get her worked up so much. "Good-bye, Miranda, I'll see you at next rehearsal."

Margaret quickly walked away, fuming, as she made her way to the parking lot.

❖

Rory spent the rest of the weekend holed up in her room, alternating between catching up on her homework and kicking herself for being such a jerk. She resisted repeated attempts from Rachel to go out again, telling her that once a semester was plenty. Rachel was disappointed but didn't harp on it and let her be. She appreciated that about Rachel. Rachel was good about knowing when you needed to be kept at arm's length and when you needed to be pulled in for a hug. This weekend, she just really needed to be by herself.

She could understand where Margaret was coming from, she really could. She knew that professors had a different standard they had to live up to; she had to be the adult and set a good example. Professors were not supposed to be dating their students or making it look as if they were. Gay and lesbian professors were under an even bigger microscope than the straight ones. Damn, there must be some schools out there that weren't as buttoned up about things as her school was.

Rory really did get the problems Margaret faced; it had just hurt in the moment to be so completely rejected. She had been able to accept the friend zone—at least it meant she got to know a side of Margaret that the other students did not. But to be back to only seeing her in the classroom or the theater? That was brutal. Maybe Margaret had meant it when she had said that once the semester was over and Rory was no longer in her class, then they could revisit the idea of being friends. It was something to look forward to.

Rory sighed. All this introspection was not getting her homework done. "I owe Margaret an apology," she muttered. She'd take care of that on Monday, after class.

Chapter Six

O n Monday, Rory did her best impression of a diligent student. She sat up most of the time, took notes, even asked and answered a question or two. The lecture was a good one. Margaret was discussing the history of the Globe Theatre, and Rory had always found it interesting. Rory was able to forget about all the BS, or as Rachel often referred to it, lesbian drama, and just enjoy herself. But when Margret announced they were done, Rory hung back so she could be the last one in the room and be able to get a moment alone with her.

Margaret didn't seem to pay Rory any mind as Rory slowly gathered her things. Margaret started to leave and Rory had to call out to her. "Dr. Parks, can I talk to you a moment?"

Margaret stopped in her tracks and faced Rory with a hesitant smile on her face, clutching to her chest the items she'd brought to class—a binder, which held her lecture notes, a book about the Globe, and some pens. "Sure, Rory, what's on your mind?"

Facing her, with her backpack slung over one shoulder, Rory could only look at her shoes. She knew she was mumbling when she said, "I'm sorry."

"What did you say?" Margaret asked.

Rory looked up into Margaret's eyes, saw the smile she was trying to hide, knew that Margaret had heard her perfectly, and smiled in return. "I said I'm sorry. I'm sorry for being such a jerk to you the other day. You didn't deserve that."

Margaret was smiling now. "I accept your apology." Margaret closed her eyes and looked down for a moment before she spoke again. When she did look up again, she looked into Rory's face and the smile was gone. "And I'm sorry for...sorry for hurting you." Rory started to protest but Margaret stopped her. "Don't disagree, I know I did, and I hope you know that was never my intention."

"I know that. What hurts the most is the thought that you don't want to be my friend, even. That being seen with me is toxic or something."

Margaret put her books on the desk rather abruptly and they made a loud noise. "Dammit, Rory, you're not toxic and I never meant to imply that. So get that out of your head." She pointed a finger at Rory's chest. "What you are is a great student, a great actress, and you were becoming a good friend." She sighed and lowered her finger and spoke more softly, without the harshness. "I know I shouldn't let people like Miranda dictate who my friends are, so I've done some thinking over the weekend and...can we be friends again?" Margaret gave her a small smile.

Rory's grin grew slowly until it was covering her face. "You mean it? You're willing to be seen with me in public?"

Margaret laughed. "Only if you behave yourself."

"Oh, well, I can't always promise that. I gotta be me."

Margaret laughed again as she picked her belongings up off the desk. "Fine. Just be you with less glitter."

Rory knew what she was really saying and felt like apologizing again but decided once more would make her sound pathetic. Instead, she went for humor. "Not a problem. I'm not gay enough for that much glitter." They laughed together as they walked out the door.

❖

The next day, Margaret was in her office catching up on her email, a never-ending activity, when she spotted one from the dean requesting her presence in his office at her earliest convenience. She hoped he wasn't going to ask her to serve on any damn committees. She was already on four this year.

She sighed. No time like the present. She picked up her desk phone and called the dean's office, getting his secretary. "Hello, Judy, it's Margaret."

"Hey, Margaret, how ya doing?"

"I'm great, Judy. Is Charles in?"

"Yes, ma'am, and he doesn't have anyone in his office right now, in case you're calling because of that email."

"I am. Do you know what this is about?"

"Not a clue. He just told me to email you and make it urgent. So it must be important."

"That sounds ominous." Judy chuckled appreciatively. "I'll be right up." Margaret locked her door and went up to the third floor to the administration office.

Judy smiled at her when she walked in. "Go on in, I told him you were coming."

"All right." Margaret crossed the plushly carpeted office to Dean Charles Louden's door and knocked out of politeness, then walked in, not sure what to expect.

"Good afternoon, Margaret. Have a seat." Charles sat behind his desk, studying something on his computer. He looked focused and intent and not happy.

Margaret took one of the gray vinyl chairs in front of his desk and sat down. They were the old-fashioned metal and vinyl covered seats that Margaret hadn't seen since she had been in high school, and she wondered where the dean had found them. Had the campus facilities staff brought them out of some dusty warehouse just for him? "What's going on, Charles?"

Charles turned from his computer and picked up a pencil. He held it in both hands for a moment and looked down at it before he spoke. "Margaret, I don't know the best way to bring this up. I've never had to do it with a woman before, and I will apologize now for bungling it." He attempted a nervous smile.

"You're as nervous as a boy about to ask his crush on a date. You're not about to do that, are you?" She smiled, trying humor with him. She couldn't think of a reason why he would be so nervous. What could he possibly want to ask her or say to her that would make him so uneasy?

He chuckled some but then composed himself. "No, no. As you know, I'm a happily married man. No, what I want to talk to you about is some disturbing information someone passed on to me."

Margaret felt her stomach drop as if she was on a roller coaster. This couldn't possibly be about Rory—they'd done nothing wrong. All they had shared was a meal or two. "What disturbing information?"

Charles cleared his throat. "Well, um…it's been reported that you have been having an inappropriate relationship with a female student, and I want to get to the bottom of these allegations."

"I don't know who you're getting your information from, but whatever you've been told is most definitely not true. I would never use my position to enhance my personal life."

"Right. My source claims that you've been…cavorting with a young woman who's your student and who you cast in your play, an Aurora Morgan. I've been sent pictures of the two of you in a compromising position."

Pictures? Of something that never happened? "Charles, I've never been in a compromising position with her or any of my students. What kind of picture could someone possibly have?" Charles turned his computer screen around and Margaret saw a photo of herself and Rory sitting at the table in the diner, and they were holding hands. Margaret knew when it had been taken: the night she and Rory had had an intimate moment across the table, before she had put an end to it. Before they'd realized Miranda was there, watching them.

"This looks compromising to me, what about you?"

"Charles, you have to believe me when I say that's not what it looks like." Even Margaret was finding that hard to believe, as she could see the tenderness in her eyes as she looked at Rory. She was just hoping she could talk her way out of this.

"I don't have to believe anything. It looks to me like you and one of your students are holding hands across a table and are looking lovingly at each other."

Margaret tried not to scoff. "What that picture shows is two people having a tender moment, yes, but it was not a romantic one." She hoped she could pull off that lie. "Just two people who were sharing personal stories. At this moment, she'd told me something that touched me and I felt compelled to reach out to her. The truth is, I think we might be becoming friends. She's a fascinating young woman and I enjoy her company." At least that part was the truth.

"You know how this looks, though, right? I don't mean to be indelicate, but you're a lesbian. And she's a student, for crying out loud."

"Charles, calling me a lesbian is not indelicate. But what you're implying is. Nothing inappropriate has ever, nor will ever, happen."

"Fine, I accept that. But you need to be careful. If her

parents find out about this, all hell could break loose. To say nothing of the media."

"And what does be careful mean to you?" Margaret fixed him with a steady look, trying not to glare.

Charles was suddenly flustered. "Well…it means don't be seen in public holding hands or doing anything else that could be deemed inappropriate."

"Well, I must confess, Charles, we did share a milk shake once. But we had different straws."

"You can't joke your way out of this, Margaret. This could turn into a serious mess. I'm not just telling you this as your boss—I'm telling you this as your friend."

Margaret barely restrained herself from laughing out loud. They had never been friends. She stood up to go. "Let's say the words, Charles. You're insinuating that I'm sexually coercing a student, or on the path to doing so. If you're really my friend, you know that I would never do what you're accusing me of and that I am capable of having adult friendships with adult students and still be professional. And that's what I'm going to continue to do." She turned and walked to the door.

Charles called out to her. "Margaret, at the very least, just think of what I'm asking as protecting your job."

Margaret stopped with one hand on the doorknob and turned to face him. "If having job security means I don't get to have the friends I want, then maybe this isn't the job for me after all."

"What are you saying, that you would leave over this?"

"I'm saying that no matter how much I love this job, and I do, make no mistake, it doesn't control me. If you persist in trying to tell me how to run my life outside of work, when I've done nothing to warrant such attention, then I will have no choice."

"I'm not trying to control you, Margaret. I just don't want

the shit to hit the fan over this." There was desperation in his voice and Margaret almost felt sorry for him.

"It'll be fine, Charles." She didn't stick around for a comeback from him. She walked out, nodded to Judy, and went back to her office, fuming. She wasn't sure who to be mad at the most: Charles for his insinuation, Miranda for tipping off the dean, or herself for allowing such an unguarded moment in public. What she was sure of was she'd meant what she said about finding a new job if they told her how to conduct her personal life.

❖

The next day, feeling defiant, Margaret called out to Rory as she was leaving class. "Hold up a minute, would you? I need to discuss something with you." A few people glanced in Rory's direction, and for a second, Margaret wondered if there were rumors floating around about the two of them.

Rory looked at her, an obvious question in her expression. "Sure, Dr. Parks." Rory made her way to the desk, backpack on one shoulder as usual.

Margaret smiled at the rest of the students as they all quickly left, then she turned to Rory with a smile. "What are you doing after this?"

"By *this*, do you mean this class, or school and the rest of my life?" Rory grinned and Margaret saw a slight twinkle in her eyes. She'd always thought that was just romantic hokum, but maybe not.

"I meant right now."

"Oh. I see. Nothing much, just going back to the room to stare at the wall…I mean, study."

"Well, if you're busy…" Margaret grinned, enjoying herself.

"No, no, nothing you couldn't tear me away from. What'd you have in mind, Doc?"

Margaret shook her head. "Oh God, not that again."

"What's wrong with *Doc*?"

"Well, first off, I don't have a medical degree. And second, it always reminds me of Bugs Bunny."

"I see. I'll have to think of a new nickname. Anyway, where'd you want to go?"

"I was thinking we could go for a stroll around the pond." Margaret knew that what she was proposing sounded like a romantic gesture and she could tell by the surprised look on Rory's face that that was how she was taking it. But Margaret was still pissed off after the conversation with the dean and didn't care what anyone thought. All she wanted to do was just get as far away from her office as she could and spend time with her friend.

"Well, it's a good day for it, pleasant weather and all. Why not?"

"Do you want to take your bag back to your room?"

"Nope, I'm good. That's why I have two shoulders." She shrugged with a grin.

"Okay, then. Let me just take this"—she indicated her binder and books—"to my office."

Rory took her bag off her shoulder and unzipped it and held out her hand. "Here, I've got room."

Margaret was immediately touched and felt herself blushing. No one had ever offered to carry her books for her before. She felt a little foolish for thinking that way, but it was still a sweet gesture. "Are you sure?"

"Yeah, plenty of room. Come on, give over."

"All right. Here." Margaret handed Rory her things and Rory had no trouble fitting them into the backpack. "Thank you."

"You're welcome. Shall we?"
"Indeed."

❖

Rory and Margaret walked to the man-made lake in the middle of the small park on the far south side of the campus. As they slowly walked around the lake, Margaret considered bringing her class out here sometime. They could do their own version of Shakespeare in the park. She smiled at the thought.

Rory walked beside her, hands casually at her sides. "I saw that smile. What's on your mind?"

Margaret stopped and looked out across the water, her hand shielding her eyes from the late-afternoon sun. "I was just thinking this would be a great place for Shakespeare."

"You mean like a Shakespeare in the park kind of thing?" Margaret nodded. "That's a great idea. Just for our class, or like a separate project?"

Margaret shrugged. "Not sure yet. Maybe start with our class and then see how it goes. If enough people seem interested, then we can open it up to everyone."

"Sounds like a good idea."

They fell into silence again and continued walking.

Margaret couldn't remember the last time she had walked around a lake with someone, friend or otherwise. She was trying to resist the strong urge she had to grab Rory's hand. She knew she couldn't pass that off as just a friendly gesture. She was tempted, but she was still stung by the accusation of impropriety and felt guilty for even having the thoughts she was having, even though, despite the encouragement from Bill and Dix to go forward and just see what happened, she had no intention of doing so.

They walked around the whole lake, which didn't take

all that long, and the conversation moved on to other topics. As the sun started to make its slow descent in the west, they stopped to watch the sunset.

"Isn't it beautiful?" Rory said. Margaret looked up at her. "I'm definitely more of a sunset girl than a sunrise girl. For starters, you don't have to get up early just to see it. But mainly because I like the deep, rich colors better." Rory was looking wistfully up at the sky. Suddenly, she reached for Margaret's hand and Margaret wasn't sure how to react.

Margaret looked at their clasped hands, then up at Rory's awestruck face and smiled. She squeezed back and took half a step closer to her, then she too looked up at the sunset. "It is. More beautiful, I mean."

Rory glanced down at her, and for a moment, Margaret thought she was going to kiss her. Instead she just looked at her, really looked at her. Margaret felt exposed and wasn't sure how to react. She was damned if she was going to break the gaze, however. She wasn't sure if that came from defiance, but she held her ground and she held Rory's attention. Finally, she came to a decision. "Are you hungry?"

Rory blinked for a moment. It seemed that she too expected something more from that moment, but she recovered quickly. "Oh...sure, I could eat. Burgers again?"

Margaret dropped her hand from Rory's and chuckled. "No. I was thinking that it must have been a while since you had a home-cooked meal, so I was thinking I could make you something. That is, if you're brave enough."

Rory grinned. "Oh, I'm brave enough. I ain't afraid of you, Doc."

"I meant my cooking."

"I guess only time will tell about that one. Lead the way."

CHAPTER SEVEN

Margaret's house was a small one-bedroom, a few blocks from campus. Since it was just her and she didn't plan on having children, she had never felt the need for anything more. Her living room was furnished with a mismatched sofa and high-backed chair, both comfortable and perfect in their differences. Margaret spent most of her time in the corner, at a small Queen Anne desk she had taken when she had moved out of her parents' house in Boston.

Margaret put her things on her desk. "Make yourself comfortable. I'm going to get something to drink before I start cooking." She eyed Rory skeptically as she placed her backpack on the floor next to the couch, then unzipped it and pulled out Margaret's things and set them on the coffee table. "Rory, how old are you again?"

Rory seemed surprised at the question. "Twenty-five, why?"

"Just making sure you're legal before I offer you a glass of wine." Margaret tried not to let herself think about the real reason she had asked.

"Oh, that's all right then. But I'll take a beer if you got it."

"Just wine, sorry. Will that be all right?"

"Sure, why not."

Margaret brought the drinks out and, after handing Rory

hers, took a seat at her desk. She noticed Rory gulped her wine, out of nervousness, she was sure. "Okay, now that I've been fortified, there probably is something we should talk about." Rory cocked an eyebrow at her but said nothing, silently urging Margaret to continue. "Do you remember the last time we were at the diner and we saw Miranda on the way out?" Rory nodded. "Well, I think she may have snapped a picture of us and sent it to the dean, who called me into his office yesterday. Or at least, someone took a picture."

"Whatever was in that picture wouldn't show anything that should get you in trouble."

"We were holding hands."

"She must have been watching us like a hawk to even catch that." Rory shook her head, looking disgusted. "I'm sorry, Margaret, I feel partly to blame for this."

Margaret set her wineglass down on a coaster on her desk and leaned forward in her chair. "Whatever for? Neither of us has done anything wrong and should not be made to feel as if we have."

"What I mean is, I know she's doing this out of revenge. She keeps asking me out and I keep saying no. She hasn't taken it very well."

Margaret was even more pissed than she had been after talking to Charles. "Then she better fucking learn how to deal with rejection if she wants to be an actress, or a mature adult, for that matter. Sorry, you can't get what you want in this world by throwing a tantrum."

Rory was chuckling. She suddenly sat up, placed her glass on the coffee table, and declared, "We need music."

"Music?" Rory's sudden change in topic caught her off guard, but she tried not to show it. "My stereo is right over there, help yourself." She gestured to a short bookcase on the other side of the room, on top of which was set a high-end stereo with a record player. The bookcase below housed her records.

"You listen to records?" Rory approached the bookcase with care, showing reverence to the collection.

"Well, I listen to big band, blues, and jazz mostly, and they only sound right on vinyl. There's just something about the sound of the needle on the vinyl that adds to the whole experience. The supposed perfection of the sound quality of CDs just can't compare to the realness of a record."

Rory smiled as she scanned the shelves. She turned to Margaret. "Who's your favorite?"

Margaret walked over to stand next to Rory at the bookcase. "My favorite? That's kind of hard to say."

"There must be one that's special, one you turn to more than the others."

"Hmm, since you put it that way..." She searched through the albums until she found the one she wanted. "This one."

Rory took it from her with a smile. "Ella Fitzgerald and Louis Armstrong. Good choice." She put the record on and selected a song, "Cheek to Cheek." Rory smiled at Margaret, then bowed. "May I have this dance?"

Amused and somewhat surprised, Margaret laughed at the invitation. "Okay, though I don't know how good I'll be, it's been a while." Maxine didn't dance and Margaret wasn't the type to go out alone. Probably the last time she had danced, she reasoned, had been when her father was still alive. He'd also liked to play his records and pull her and her mother into dancing with him.

Rory took Margaret in her arms and swayed with her to the fun beat. Rory fell naturally into leading; Margaret didn't mind. They were having fun, putting their cheeks together. They danced to one song, then another, and then Rory selected another album and took Margaret back in her arms.

She relaxed into Rory's embrace, letting herself be led. It felt natural, as if they were used to dancing together. And she was having fun dancing in her living room…with her student. Just as she was starting to hesitate about the wisdom of what she was doing, the song switched to something slower, one of her favorites, "A Kiss to Build a Dream On," and Rory drew her closer. She knew she shouldn't be enjoying this as much as she was, but she couldn't help it.

Rory sighed in pleasure, and then she looked down and started singing directly to Margaret.

As Rory was singing, imploring for a kiss, Margaret forgot all the reasons they shouldn't. They were no longer teacher and student, but two people caught up in a moment filled with emotion and attraction. As their lips came together, they stopped dancing and Rory put one hand on the side of Margaret's face, while Margaret put both arms around Rory's waist.

Rory's lips were soft and tasted of the wine, as Margaret was sure hers did too. She lost herself for a moment, as their tongues played with each other and she let out a small moan. She threaded her fingers through Rory's belt loops and pulled her closer still. She was about to guide Rory the few steps over to the couch when her brain suddenly started working again. She pulled away abruptly and stepped back, letting go of Rory entirely.

"What's wrong?" Rory took a step toward her but Margaret held up a hand.

"Stop. We shouldn't do this. We can't do this. I'm sorry, it's my fault, I should have known better. I'm sorry."

"We haven't done anything wrong, we're both consenting adults."

"I know, but I'm still your professor."

"Then I'll drop the class. Margaret, I really like you and

I think you like me too." She tried taking a step forward again and this time Margaret didn't stop her but she didn't move toward her either.

"Rory, I'm sorry, this can't happen. I think you should go." She was nearly whispering. She didn't want to hurt her again.

Instead of leaving, Rory took another step closer, but Margaret held her ground. Rory reached out to Margaret and gently brushed a stray hair off Margaret's face, then let her fingers fall into a caress. "Just think about it. Think about how that kiss felt, not what your brain is telling you. Don't dismiss this." Rory held Margaret's gaze with her hand still resting on Margaret's cheek. Margaret sighed, then looked down, shaking her head. Rory backed away. "You know there's something there, you're just afraid of it. Don't be. It just might be the best thing to happen to both of us. It just might be beautiful." Rory picked up her backpack, put it on one shoulder, took one last look at Margaret, then walked out the door.

Margaret covered her face with her hands and muttered to herself, "Oh, Parks, you are in so much trouble."

❖

After Rory left, Margaret sat at her desk, in a bit of a state of shock. There was no doubt she had enjoyed the kiss. The problem was that she knew she shouldn't have. It was the line that she had told herself and the dean that she wouldn't cross. "Well, so much for integrity," she said to the empty room. She just wasn't sure what to do about it. She knew Rory had a point; there was something there between them. And it might just be beautiful. But she wasn't sure if she could take the risk.

She sighed and decided she needed to get her mind off it for a while. She checked her email. Among the student emails, there was yet another email from the dean. She opened it with dread. The first thing she saw was a picture of herself and Rory staring into each other's eyes, as they held hands in front of a lovely sunset. "What the fuck, is that girl hiding in bushes now?" Below the picture, was a terse message from the dean: *This stops now.*

Incensed, Margaret quickly closed out her email. Son of a bitch. She put her head in her hands for a moment. She wasn't sure she could even wrap her mind around all that had just happened in the past twenty-four hours. She and Rory had a stalker and an enraged dean on their ass—all this before they'd had any real intimate contact. What pissed her off the most was the audacity of the dean, who thought he had a right to tell her what to do. She hadn't done anything wrong, and yet, she felt chastised and persecuted, all at the same time. How dare he?

"Hell, I might as well, he already thinks I am." Suddenly feeling devilish, she pulled out her phone and texted Bill: *I'm about to find out what-if. Wish me luck.*

Bill's response came back: *OMG, go get her and good luck, honey.*

Before she could think about it too much and talk herself out of it, she smiled, then texted Rory: *If I haven't ruined things completely, would you consider coming back? We never finished our dance.*

The next two minutes were agonizing while she waited for the reply.

You're right about that. Or the kissing.

Margaret let a small smile escape. *Or the kissing. Now get your ass over here.*

The reply was instantaneous. *Yes, ma'am.*

Ten minutes later, there was a knock on the door. Margaret opened it with a smile on her face. It was now dark out and a somewhat out of breath Rory stood on her porch, her red curls silhouetted under the porch light. Her face bore a nervous smile.

"I'm not making any promises," Margaret declared.

"I'm not asking you to. I just want to spend time with you. Whatever happens, happens. Can I come in?" There was hesitation in her voice, and Margaret understood it perfectly. She felt the same way.

She grabbed Rory's hand and pulled her inside and over to the couch, where they sat facing each other. "Rory, there's something I should tell you."

"Sounds serious." Rory brushed a strand of hair from Margaret's face.

Margaret sighed from the pleasure of the touch. "Stop distracting me." Smiling, Rory dropped her hand. "Before we decide to go any further with this, I think it's only fair to tell you about the consequences."

"Didn't we discuss this earlier?"

"Somewhat. But there are some very real consequences that could happen if you and I engage in…a more personal relationship, and I want to make you aware of them."

Rubbing Margaret's leg, Rory smiled and said, "Yeah, like you could fall in love with me."

Margaret put her hand on Rory's to stop the motion. "Besides that, smart-ass. My contract has a morals clause, and having an affair with a student, even a grad student, triggers a lot of red flags."

Turning serious, Rory asked, "Could you be fired?"

"It's possible. My authority over you in the classroom could be read as coercing a sexual relationship."

Looking gloomy, Rory said, "No wonder you've been resistant. I would be too. I can back off if that's what you want."

Knowing an out when she heard one, Margaret knew she could take Rory up on her offer and put a stop to this before it got out of control. Before she lost her heart. But one look at the look of loss and acceptance already forming on Rory's face and Margaret knew they were already past the point of no return. Basking in the heat of her nearness, she said, "I have spent my life doing what I should. I went to the right school, took a sensible job, and had proper relationships. Do you know what I haven't had?"

"What?"

"Fun. Passion. Excitement. I think it's time to remedy that, don't you?"

"If that's what you want."

"More than anything."

Rory gently leaned in and softly kissed Margaret's waiting lips. Margaret put a hand on the back of Rory's head and the other at Rory's waist, resting her fingers on Rory's belt. She opened her mouth to receive Rory's searching tongue, then played with it. When Rory withdrew, Margaret took possession of Rory's bottom lip, sucking it into her mouth for several moments before releasing it.

Rory pulled back. "I could do this all night."

"Who's stopping you?" Margaret trailed kisses from the tip of Rory's ear to her collarbone. "I want to make out with you on my couch tonight. Nothing more, nothing less. I hope you're okay with that." Margaret began to suck on Rory's ear.

"Maybe I should go so we're not tempted to do more than this." Rory made no attempt to move as Margaret kept nibbling on her earlobe.

Margaret whispered in her ear, "Don't you dare get off this couch."

Rory laughed. "There you go, using your authority over me. Shame on you."

"I wouldn't want to do that."

"Nope." Laughing together, they resumed their previous activity.

Despite the difficulty, they both managed to keep their clothes on. Margaret mused that she still had some boundaries left. Eventually, she reluctantly made Rory get up and she drove her back to campus. They didn't kiss good night, fearing it would make them start everything all over again.

"I'll see you tomorrow," Rory said, when they reached her dorm.

"I'll see you tomorrow. Good night, Rory." She drove away with the taste of Rory still on her tongue. How the hell would she get through rehearsal?

Chapter Eight

Before rehearsal the next day, Rory found herself whistling and, once, even singing, "A Kiss to Build a Dream On." She was being so sappy and sickening that she could barely stand herself. When Rachel came by, she was blaring Louis Armstrong in an effort to exorcise the song from her head.

"Since when do you listen to old-timey music?" Rachel made herself comfortable on Rory's bed, and Rory, who had been sitting at her desk working on a paper, turned to face her.

Rory couldn't contain a grin. "This is not old-timey music, it's Louis Armstrong, you simpleton."

"What's with your face? Is that a smile?"

"You've seen them before."

"But on you, it's been a while. What happened since I saw you last?"

Rory said nothing, just shrugged and kept a goofy grin on her face.

"If I didn't know any better, I'd say you got laid. But the Aurora Morgan I know doesn't do that sort of thing." Rachel tapped Rory's shoe with her own. "So what's up, buttercup? Why the old love songs and the goofy grin?"

"I did not get laid."

"But you got close, didn't you?"

"Maybe—and that's all I'm going to say."

"Who was it? The last I heard you had been rejected."

"Well, she changed her mind. Now, leave so I can get some more work done before rehearsal."

"Are you ever going to tell me who this girl is? Why are you being so secretive?"

Rory pretended to hesitate. "Well, you *have* been a good friend. And you do live vicariously through me…"

"I do not! I get plenty of action on my own, thank you very much."

"I know, you're the talk of Cellblock C." Cellblock C was the campus nickname for their dorm.

"If I'm the slut of Clements Hall, then you're the nun."

"Alas, we must each play our part. Besides, I'm 'bout to drop this nun thing like a bad habit." Rory couldn't help but grin as Rachel rolled her eyes.

"Oh, the pun damage, it hurts." Rachel pretended to clutch her chest for a moment. "Careful, you might turn into one of those douches who brag about their conquests."

"I wouldn't want to take that away from you."

"That's it, I'm out of here. There are plenty of other places I can go to be insulted."

Rory bent her head back to what she had been doing before Rachel showed up. "Okay, have fun."

"You too, Sister Aurora."

"Thanks, douche. Hugs and kisses."

❖

Margaret arrived to rehearsal a few minutes early and wasn't surprised to see that there were only a few cast members scattered about. She was happy to see Arenda, her stage manager, in her usual seat up front. She was not happy to see Miranda sitting on the edge of the stage, legs dangling over the edge, phone in her hand, head bent, texting someone. For Margaret, the worst part of getting through rehearsal was not going to be acting as if nothing had happened with Rory the night before but, rather, treating Miranda as if she didn't know it had most likely been her who had sent the pictures to the dean. How was she supposed to be neutral about it? She just wasn't sure.

After a minute, Miranda stopped texting, put her phone in her pocket, and looked up at Margaret. Miranda gave her what appeared to be a genuine smile, but Margaret couldn't help but find it sinister. She tried to remind herself that she could be wrong about the pictures. It was possible someone else sent them. The question was, who? And why? Miranda was the most obvious candidate, as she had motive and means, for the first one for sure. For the time being, Margaret decided to ignore her and took her seat next to Arenda.

Rory came in a couple minutes later and took the seat across the aisle from Margaret as was her habit and stretched her long legs out in front of her. She rested the script on her lap and clasped her hands together across the chair arms, the picture of casual cool.

Margaret saw Rory come in and take her seat but didn't glance up again, no matter how much she wanted to. Instead, she kept her head bent and her back turned talking to Arenda. But that didn't mean that she wasn't completely aware of Rory back there. Besides Rory's cologne, which was something musky and masculine, Margaret was picking up on her overall nearness. Maybe she was romanticizing things a bit, but she couldn't help but think they were somehow connected now in a way she couldn't explain. Dear Lord, she was losing her head over one little make-out session on her couch. What the hell was wrong with her? This was definitely not like her at all. And she kinda liked it.

She didn't hazard a glance in Rory's direction until it was time to start rehearsal. She did so casually and barely let her gaze fall on her, but in that brief moment, Rory gave her a smile that was more than just casual and bored, more than a normal smile from a student to a teacher. Margaret felt a blush rise on her cheeks and silently cursed her Irish heritage for making her emotions so quick to come to the surface.

"Okay, today we're doing the dinner table scene, so I need everyone onstage."

Everyone slowly removed themselves from wherever they had been lounging and began to take their places. Rory took a moment to send a text to Margaret; she didn't want to be seen or overheard saying what she was going to say. *Maggie, that's what I shall call you. You're the real Maggie the cat.* Then, making sure the ringer was off, she slipped her phone in her pocket and stood up with her script to take her place on stage among her fellow actors. She figured she could fake being civil to Miranda, but that would be her biggest acting challenge to date. She watched Margaret put her hand in her pocket and pull out her phone. She saw the small smile creep up on her face and the blush in her cheeks. She liked knowing that she was the cause.

Margaret typed something, and then put her phone back in her pocket. "All right, begin."

Rory knew she wasn't supposed to pull her phone out while onstage, but it wasn't her turn to talk yet. *Shame on you for reading this now. Maggie it is, though I'm not a cat. And I jumped off the roof. So I'm just your Maggie.* Rory knew she was blushing at this point. Her Maggie. She liked the sound of that. Instead of replying, she looked at Maggie and gave her a small smile and an even smaller nod. Maggie locked eyes with her for a moment, but only a moment.

Rory took her eyes off Maggie and tuned in to what was happening on the stage, so she wouldn't miss her cue. She caught Miranda looking directly at her; when Miranda realized Rory had caught her staring, she cocked an eyebrow at her. Rory wasn't sure what she meant by that and didn't want to read too much into it. Instead, she gave her a questioning look, and Miranda gestured with her head in Maggie's direction, then gave Rory a slight knowing nod. Rory immediately became pissed at Miranda's audacity and presumption and the fact that she seemed to be flaunting the knowledge she thought she had. That incensed Rory enough that she missed her cue and Davis had to prompt her.

He whispered to her, "Honey, you're up."

Rory jumped back into reality, embarrassed that she had let herself be distracted enough to miss a cue.

❖

Friday, before class began, Maggie was in her office working on an article she was submitting to a theater journal, when there was a knock on her closed door. Her office hours had ended a couple hours before and she had closed her door so she could get some work done. She thought about ignoring the knock.

"Margaret, are you in there?"

It was Charles. She briefly entertained the notion of ignoring him but sighed. She wasn't the type of person to do that. She hollered out, "It's open, Charles."

Charles was less than pleased. He practically slammed her door and did not take a seat. "Margaret, I trust you've seen my email?"

"Yes, I did." She rolled her chair back and turned it so

she could lean it against the wall. Standing, he had a clear height advantage, and Maggie wondered if he was doing it on purpose.

"Margaret, I thought you understood me."

"And I thought you understood me, Charles."

"Meaning?"

"Meaning, that who I'm friends with is none of your concern."

"Friends? Pictures don't lie. One, maybe, you can pass off with some weak story, but not two. You lied to me. You stood right in my office and lied to me."

"Charles, I didn't lie to you."

"What, are you trying to tell me that you were *twice* caught up in a moment and ended up holding hands? Because I find that absurd."

"I find it absurd that you're getting this upset over hand-holding, since there's nothing improper in either picture. It's not as if a sex tape surfaced."

Charles's face went white. "Don't even joke about that. Is that something I have to be worried about now too?"

Maggie's first response was anger but considering that she and Rory had spent the last two nights making out on her couch, she let her righteous indignation go. Calmly, she said, "No, Charles, that won't happen."

"Yeah, those pictures shouldn't have happened either, but they did." Charles calmed down some and finally took a seat. "Margaret, can I be honest with you?"

Surprised by his change in tone, she softened her own and said, "By all means."

"Margaret, I don't give a good goddamn what you do. If you're shtupping this student and she's consenting, I personally couldn't care less. But I know what an affair like this could lead to if it gets out. It wouldn't be good for anyone.

And you would take the fallout. The girl would be seen as an innocent victim and you a predator. That's just the way it is. I know, time was, a man could sleep with as many students as he wanted and no one would bat an eye, it was almost expected. Even men aren't getting away unscathed these days." Charles looked wistful, as if he wished for the return of the times he spoke of. "And it's even worse for women, whether gay or straight. I just don't want this to blow up in our faces."

When she realized that he wasn't really concerned for her, but for how much it would affect him, her anger rose up again. She spoke evenly. "I don't want that either, Charles."

"Does this mean that you're not going to see her anymore?"

"I never said I was seeing her in the first place, and even if I am, the answer would be no. Whatever type of relationship Ms. Morgan and I have is our business. Not yours or anyone else's." Maggie turned back around to face her computer. "Now, if you'll excuse me, I have to prepare for class."

"The class with her in it?"

Without missing a beat, she said, "Yes. And nineteen other students, none of whom I've slept with either."

"No need to be crass about it." Charles stood up to leave. "Just think about what I've said and be careful." With that, what Maggie hoped was his final declaration on the subject, Charles left.

Maggie sat there for a moment, fighting her anger. She had always had a defiant streak in her when told she couldn't do something she wanted to do, especially when there was no real, good reason why she shouldn't. Often, she ignored the inclination to rebel, but every now and again it became too difficult to ignore.

Sitting next to her on the desk was the stack of graded papers she was going to be handing back during today's class. She pulled Rory's from the pile. She had already written her comments on the title page, but she added something to that: *See note on inside title page.* Then, she flipped that page over and wrote, *Bring an overnight bag to rehearsal and tell your family you love them, because I'm going to keep you for myself tonight and may not let you go.* Smiling to herself, she put the paper back in the stack, gathered the rest of her things, and headed to class.

Once everyone started trickling in, Maggie began to pass back the papers. As usual, most of the students immediately checked their grade and read the comments. Some students didn't seem to care, just shoved the papers in their bags and ignored them. She handed Rory hers and walked on, not facing her, so as not to make eye contact, as she had found that just looking at Rory now could bring a blush to her cheeks.

As she walked to the next row, she heard Rory let out a surprised laugh, and when Maggie looked in her direction, she saw her covering her mouth with her hand in an effort not to laugh out loud again. "Did I write something funny, Ms. Morgan?"

The rest of the class chuckled at the situation, especially since Rory was still trying to hold back her laughter. She replied, "No, no, you didn't. Got a better grade than I expected, is all."

"I see. Well, if you get an A on the final, please try to contain yourself."

There was more laughter and Rory bit her lip.

"Yes, Dr. Parks."

Despite her resolve to avoid eye contact with Rory, Maggie felt her cheeks getting hot from the thought of spending the weekend with Rory. To say she couldn't wait was an understatement.

CHAPTER NINE

Rory packed her overnight bag, then headed out to rehearsal with butterflies in her stomach. Once at rehearsal, she was only half there, as all she could think about was *after* rehearsal. Maggie had texted that she would pick Rory up in the same spot near her dorm she had dropped her off the last time they had gone out for burgers. Rory knew it was because they couldn't be seen leaving together and wasn't sure how to feel about the seeming illicitness of the whole thing.

She tried to act casual after rehearsal, even stopping to talk to a couple of her castmates for a few minutes, constantly aware out of the corner of her eye that Maggie was still in the theater, acting just as casual as she was. When she saw Maggie finally gather her things and leave, she chatted for another minute or two, then she walked out as well, making sure she didn't rush. She saw Maggie's car parked in roughly the same spot as before and jogged up to it. She opened the door with a smile on her face. "Hey."

"Get in." As Rory got in, Maggie tried to keep the grin off her face when she said, "You didn't have to run. I would have waited."

"You didn't have to pick me up. I would have run all the way to your house."

"Duly noted."

Once they got to Maggie's house, they didn't say anything as they made their way to the front door. Maggie unlocked the door and stepped in, with Rory following close behind. Maggie closed the door behind her. Once the door closed and before Maggie could say anything more, Rory dropped her backpack on the floor, put her hands on either side of Maggie's waist, and pushed her up against the wall. Maggie's arms went around Rory's neck, and she had time for a small smile before Rory's mouth found hers.

Rory's hands explored Maggie's body, as Maggie let hers find purchase in Rory's curls. As Rory was trailing her lips from Maggie's ear to her neck, Maggie suddenly gripped a handful of Rory's hair and pulled her away. Rory looked at her questioningly. Maggie gave her a small nod and said just one word. "Now."

Rory didn't need any more encouragement. She picked Maggie up by the waist and lifted her off the ground. Maggie squealed in delight and immediately wrapped her legs around Rory's waist, her arms around Rory's neck.

Laughing, Maggie said, "Don't you dare drop me."

"Not a chance. Don't worry, I've got you." Planting a kiss on Maggie's lips, Rory began to make her way to Maggie's bedroom.

Thankfully, the door was open as Rory carried her into the room and to the bed, gently setting her down. Maggie pulled Rory down on top of her, putting her arms around Rory's neck, and resumed kissing her.

There had been a moment, when Maggie had said that it was time, that Rory felt some doubt. She had never had sex with a woman before—or anyone, for that matter—and wanted to make sure she did everything right. But realizing that she couldn't let doubt take over, she went with her instincts, and her instincts told her to touch Maggie where she would want to be touched. So once they were on the bed, Rory very gently pulled away Maggie's blouse, then slid her hands under Maggie's bra and released her breasts, putting her lips on Maggie's eager nipple. She sucked gently at first, running her tongue over the tip, then nibbled and bit until Maggie moaned and squirmed under her and grabbed her curls in a tight grip. Rory couldn't help it, she laughed. To know that she could give that much pleasure to Maggie, that she was the cause of Maggie arching her back and pushing Rory's face into her breast, was a heady feeling. Rory built on that feeling and it ignited her own passion, as she went from one nipple to the other, kissing and sucking and biting all the way across, until she trailed her kisses gently down Maggie's stomach and all the way down to the button on Maggie's pants. Rory pulled back enough to undo the button and slid the zipper down, and Maggie helped Rory take her pants off. Once Maggie was resettled, Rory resumed the light touches and trailed her lips down to Maggie's clit, where she licked and sucked with more vigor than she had shown Maggie's nipples.

"Oh God, yes!"

Maggie bucked and Rory reached up with both hands and gently held Maggie's wrists to the bed while she licked her way around her labia and clit. She let her tongue dart in and out, then she freed her right hand so she could slip two fingers in, as she kept licking Maggie's clit while she slid her fingers in and out.

"Don't stop, don't stop."

Letting Maggie's passion take her over, Rory picked up speed and slid in a third finger, sliding up to give Maggie another kiss, the whole time keeping pace with her fingers with the rhythm of Maggie's body. Maggie furiously grabbed her and kissed her back, her passion hitting its crescendo.

Maggie cried out, "Yes, yes!" Then she lay back on the

pillows as Rory slowed her hand, then gently removed her fingers. She leaned down and kissed Maggie on the lips. Maggie returned her kiss, then snuggled into Rory's embrace and put her arms around her.

"Oh my God, Rory, that was wonderful."

"Really? Because I wasn't sure I could please you." Rory reveled in the praise, even though she thought it hadn't lasted nearly long enough. But Maggie did seem satisfied. "You're my first, Maggie."

"For someone who's never slept with a woman before, you seemed to know what you were doing."

"See what you've been missing?"

"What was I thinking?"

"You were thinking that you would make me practically beg for it."

"I don't recall any begging."

"No, turned out I didn't have to after all."

Maggie chuckled then turned serious. "Oh, my dear, I'm so glad to be the first one you shared this gift with. I don't feel worthy." Maggie reached up and gave Rory a sweet kiss.

"I never thought of it as a gift before, but I'm glad I waited for you. You were the right person to give it to." In that moment, Rory realized she wasn't talking about the gift of her virginity, but her heart.

Maggie, picking up on the seriousness of Rory's tone, sensed she was saying more than her words let on, and leaned her head back and looked her lover in the eyes. "Rory, everything about you is a gift I didn't know I needed until you were here. How can I say thank you for coming into my life?"

Rory blushed and looked at her questioningly.

"I think I have an idea." Maggie grinned, then bent her head to Rory's nipple and, instead of the light touch that Rory had used, gave it a bite that made Rory's whole body come awake. Rory rolled her head back and moaned out loud, encouraging Maggie as she worked on Rory's nipple. She wanted to make this special for Rory—it was her first time. She slowed down and began to pay attention to Rory's whole body, kissing and nibbling and licking her way across Rory's chest and stomach, while her hands explored the rest of Rory's long body. Her fingers brushed along Rory's long legs, up the inside of her thigh, teased her clit by lightly flicking it, then moving on. Rory groaned in protest. Maggie reached up and began sucking on Rory's right ear and firmly grabbed Rory's ass, kneading it with both hands. Rory squirmed under all this attention. Maggie took one hand off Rory's ass in order to grab that leg and pull it over her body and Rory responded by gripping Maggie tightly. Maggie kissed Rory on the mouth, letting her tongue play against Rory's in a feverish dance. Rory put her hand on the back of Maggie's head and Maggie climbed on top of her. Maggie gave Rory a final long kiss, then moved down Rory's long body until she reached her clit, and pulled it into her mouth, sucking hard on the tip, which she knew would send those thousands of nerve endings into hyperactivity.

Rory cried out her pleasure.

Then Maggie stopped sucking and began to lick, darting her tongue rapidly in and out, and then began sucking again. As she slid her fingers in slowly, Rory moaned again, put her hands on the back of Maggie's head, and lifted herself a bit in order to push herself even further into Maggie.

As Maggie worked her magic, Rory couldn't help but feel that no matter how great it was, she wanted more. She didn't want the sensations to end but she also wanted there to be some way they could merge more completely, almost melt together. As Maggie picked up speed, the only thought Rory knew was what her body was telling her, and her body was telling her only good things and it wanted more, more, more. As Maggie's actions grew in intensity and as her fingers slid in and out faster and harder, Rory couldn't stay still, and she couldn't hold back any longer. As her body shook with orgasm after orgasm, she cried out, "Yes! Yes! Oh God, yes!" and arched up one final time before collapsing back on the bed exhausted, limp all over. Even though Maggie had stopped her ministrations and had come up to wrap Rory in her arms, Rory still shook from the very intense orgasm, and she clung to Maggie like a person drowning and tried to catch her breath. Maggie caressed her curls and kissed her forehead. Finally, after several moments, when Rory could finally speak, she smiled and said, "You're going to have to work hard to top that next time, Doc."

Maggie chuckled lightly in response. "After all that, you still call me by that infernal nickname. What's a girl got to do?"

"Just keep doing that."

"Oh, I intend to."

"Good."

❖

Rory and Maggie spent the rest of that night and most of the next morning in bed, making love, only getting out to find food or take a shower before they had to go to rehearsal. At times, Maggie tried to think like an adult and insisted on getting some sleep. When she would push Rory away, begging tiredness, she felt guilty about it, but she could only go on so long before sleep overtook her. When she woke up in the middle of the night, Rory was still holding her against her chest, sleeping peacefully.

When the sun came up, Rory was sitting up in bed, rubbing the sleep out of her eyes.

Maggie looked at her and smiled. "Well, good morning, Aurora."

Rory eyed her skeptically. "Were you making a pun or just using the infernal name, Doc?"

Maggie laughed. "Take it as you will. Anyway, I suppose we should get up now."

"If we must. But I kind of like it here. I may not want to leave."

"Hmm. Should I keep a long-legged young redhead as a pet? Definitely something to consider."

"Definitely. I've had all my shots and I'm housebroken. And I only bite when and where you like it." She grinned and leaned into Maggie for a lingering kiss.

After a long moment, Maggie pulled away. "No, not again, not right now. I really must get out of bed." With that, she threw off the covers and stood up, showing she meant what she said.

Staying where she was, Rory grew serious. "You know today's Saturday, right?"

Maggie was at her closet, looking for clothes to wear. Absentmindedly, she said, "Yes, I do. What's your point?"

"Just that we have to go to rehearsal today and act like nothing ever happened."

Maggie thought about it. "I know. It has crossed my mind. It's going to be difficult, standing in the front of the room, the whole time looking at you and wanting to just suck your face…or other areas. Not that it hasn't been difficult already. But still, you do bring up an excellent point."

"That's why I've been thinking. I think I need to drop your class. Honestly, I love the play too much to drop that and it's not like I'm getting graded for it, so there's no conflict of interest there. I just don't think it would be fair for either of us."

"I want to tell you to reconsider, but I know you're right."

"And next semester I probably shouldn't take any of your grad classes either, assuming we're still together, that is." Rory seemed suddenly shy.

"Of course we'll still be together next semester. Why wouldn't we?"

Rory shrugged. "I just wasn't sure if you would still want me around by then."

"Oh, honey, I am not the love 'em and leave 'em type. I hope you know that."

"I think I do, it's just nice to hear you say it, I guess."

Instead of pulling her into her arms like she wanted to do, first Maggie needed to clear some things up, so she stayed where she was in front of the closet and crossed her arms in front of her. "Aurora Morgan, I want you to listen to what I have to say, hmm?" Rory nodded. "Despite what I had told myself from the moment we sat across from each other at the diner and you made it clear how you felt, I have not regretted a single moment since then. Yes, I was nervous. I had a lot of good reasons to be." She gave Rory a small smile and Rory looked somewhat relieved. "But despite all of that, I really care about you. This wasn't just sex for me. I want you in my life, not just now, but for a long time. Now, is that clear?" She stepped over to the bed and grabbed Rory by the chin and pulled her face closer.

"Yeah, it's clear. I feel the same way. I just didn't want to presume. You did say no promises." Rory shrugged sheepishly.

Maggie gave her a small smile and shook her head, then leaned in closer to look in Rory's eyes. They were quiet a moment, just looking. Then Rory leaned in and lightly licked the tip of Maggie's nose and pulled away, chuckling.

Maggie couldn't help but join her, as she wiped off her nose. "You're impossible."

"I think the word you're looking for is adorable."

"Yes, well, I'm hungry." Maggie stood back from the bed and went to the closet to find some clothes to put on in order to go into the kitchen to find food.

"I see how you are. You—"

"What are you about to call me?" Maggie tried to look menacing and failed.

"Ah…you gorgeous woman."

"Come on, sweet-talker, make me something edible to eat."

❖

They got through rehearsal as quickly as they could, then went through the same ritual as the night before, only Rory had to made a quick stop back at her dorm for another change of clothes. There were several people roaming the hall, loudly discussing their plans for the evening, many going through the rituals of shower and makeup and clothes selection. Rory just shook her head, glad she had never gotten caught up in all that feminine prep work. She was definitely a jeans and T-shirt kind of girl. There was no indecision or planning involved. And she knew she always looked good in a plain white shirt, faded jeans, and engineer boots. It was kind of her thing and she pulled it off, with the boots making her almost six feet tall. And bulletproof, she thought.

She made it back to Maggie's waiting car and they returned to Maggie's tiny house, where they spent the rest of the weekend, until Monday morning when they had to face the real world again and return to their normal lives.

When she stepped off the elevator on her floor after having said good-bye to Maggie, she chuckled to herself that this was her first walk of shame, though she didn't feel shame. Not at all. She felt awesome.

As she walked by the communal bathroom on her way to her room, Rachel came out wearing only an oversized flannel shirt and boxers, her long blond hair sleep-disheveled.

Rory whistled. "Mornin', Rach—nice legs."

Rachel turned sleepy eyes in Rory's direction, her gaze lingering on Rory's backpack. "And where have you been? I know you don't have class this early."

Rory walked up to Rachel and folded down the collar of her shirt, then kissed her on the cheek. "I, my friend, have been to paradise."

"Ugh, don't kiss me if your mouth has been where I think it has." Rachel wiped her cheek then smiled. "I want to hear all about it, but I'm not awake enough for this conversation. I'm going back to bed. We can talk in a couple or three hours." Rachel turned to go back to her room.

"Like you're going to be able to sleep now."

Rachel stopped in her tracks and turned around. "You're probably right. Fine, make me some coffee and tell me a bedtime story."

Rory led the way to her room and Rachel shuffled along behind her. She made an immediate beeline to Rory's bed as soon as the door was open.

"Hey, don't fall asleep yet." Rory set her bag down and went to her coffeepot to start making the promised coffee.

"Wouldn't dream of it." As she was saying this, Rachel was snuggling in and pulling the covers up around herself.

With her eyes closed, she said, "So who had the privilege of popping your cherry?"

"Rude." Rory finished making coffee and came over to the side of her bed. Rachel scooted closer to the wall and Rory sat down, legs out in front herself. "I can't tell you everything, at least not yet, but for the sake of reference, her name is Maggie." Rory felt safe giving Rachel that much information, since no one else thought of Maggie by that nickname.

"Such a nice Irish name." Rachel snuggled closer and draped an arm over Rory's legs.

"Sounds like something my mother would say." Rory absentmindedly let her hands rest on Rachel's.

"Um-hmm. Tell Mama all about this Maggie."

"Okay, that's just disturbing." Rachel said nothing. "What I can tell you is that she's kinda short, brunette, brilliant. She thinks I'm funny. I get the impression she takes herself too seriously but she lets herself go with me. I think she loves me. I know I love her."

"Aw, my baby's growing up."

"Fuck you."

"Not right now, I'm too tired. And you need a shower. For some reason you smell like vanilla. Is she a baker or something?"

Rory chuckled. Maggie's scent was lavender and vanilla. "No. Coffee's done."

"Too late for that now. I'm not long for this world."

"I knew I shouldn't have let you lie down." Rory stood up, pulled the cover up to Rachel's chin, then leaned down and kissed her on the forehead. "Night, night."

After pouring herself a cup of coffee, Rory pulled up the school's enrollment website on her laptop and did the right thing and dropped Maggie's class, then texted Maggie.

Two things: Class dropped. And Rachel (aka, Goldilocks) is sleeping in my bed. My fault, I told her a story and she fell asleep. Haven't touched her except to tuck her in, honest!

Maggie's reply came back promptly: *Thanks for telling me. Baby, I trust you.*

Breathing a sigh of relief, Rory sent one more text before she went to take a shower: *See you at rehearsal Thursday.*

CHAPTER TEN

B y the time Rachel woke up, Rory was sitting on the floor with her back propped up against the side of the bed, with a pillow between herself and the bed frame and her long legs stretched out before her. She was engrossed in reading for her theater history class when she heard Rachel groan and began to move.

"Rory?"

Without looking up, she said, "Yes, Rachel?"

"Why are you on my floor?"

"I'm not. You're in my bed."

"I am?"

"Yes."

"Why are you down there?"

"Because I'm doing my impression of a gentleman."

Suddenly sitting up, Rachel shouted, "Oh my God, you had sex!"

"Calm down, I don't think they heard you downstairs."

"Don't be ridiculous, I'm sure they did." Rachel threw the covers off and put her feet on the floor. She nudged Rory in the shoulder and held her fist out, and Rory bumped it with a wry smile. "Way to go, welcome to the club."

"There's a club? No one told me there was a club."

"Oh, yeah. We meet once a month to get drunk, eat chocolate, and bay at the moon."

"Well, sign me up for that." Rory closed her book with a pop and stood. "You *are* allowed to leave and put pants on, you know?" She set the book on her desk and then leaned against it with her arms crossed over her chest.

"Pants are overrated. Besides, do you know what people are going to think when they see me walk out of here dressed like this?" Rachel's eyes danced mischievously.

"I thought they already thought we were sleeping together."

"Yes, but now they'll think they caught us."

Rory considered this. "This is true. Fuck it, let them think what they want."

"Ooh, I love it when you talk dirty."

Rory stuck out her tongue.

"So, tell me more about Maggie."

"So, you were listening."

"Kinda."

"Well"—Rory pulled out the desk chair and sat down—"I can't tell you everything."

"Me, your best friend? Why can't you tell me everything?"

"Because some things are none of your business."

"I find that hard to believe."

"Yeah, I know." Rory sighed. "I can't say much more than I already have. I care about her a lot and I think she feels the same. She could be the one." Rory let a small smile escape.

Rachel waved her hand in a dismissive gesture. "Oh, we always think that after the first time, that's normal, it'll pass. Tell me something important, like, what does she look like?"

"Well, I categorically disagree with that—I don't expect this feeling to pass. As for what she looks like…well, you know I have a type, right?"

"Yeah, and it's not me—go on."

"Right. Well, she's not physically my type at all."

"If you're about to tell me you're dating a girl that looks like me, I'm going to slug you, you know that, right?"

"Chill, slugger, she doesn't look like you either. She's shorter than you, has long brown hair, and is a bit older than me."

"Older? By how much?"

"About fifteen years."

"Dude, that's seriously old."

"Fuck off, she's only forty."

Rachel suddenly grinned. "An older woman, you say? I bet she knows a thing or two, if you know what I mean."

"Blatant innuendo like that, my dead grandmother knows what you mean. And let's just say, she is not unskilled." Rory could feel the blush creeping up.

"Ooh, a double negative. She must be fantastic."

"Can we move on, please?"

"Aw, is this making you uncomfortable, sweetie?"

"A little."

"Okay." Pause. "So, do you have hickeys in unmentionable places? If so, I wanna see."

"All right, that's it, I'm done." Rory threw her door open and stood aside. "It's time for you to go home now, I'm done with you." She winked at Rachel, who grinned as she got up from the bed and walked to the open door.

"Just like that? You're done with me?"

"For now. I'll call you later—maybe."

"You're such an ass." Rachel huffed out of the room into the hallway, where two of her friends were hanging out in their doorway, making it no secret that they were listening. Rachel turned around, threw her arms around Rory's neck, and said, "But you know I can't say no to you." Then she kissed her on the cheek.

Rory returned the embrace and whispered in her ear, "You are so dead."

Rachel pulled away with a giggle. "Oh, you say the sweetest things, love. See you later." She gave a little wave as she walked away. When she passed her friends, she nodded to them. "Ladies." Then, just before she entered her room, she turned and blew a kiss to Rory, who slammed her door, amidst Rachel's giggles.

❖

Class without Rory was going to be ordinary, Maggie thought, Monday morning after Rory had gone back to her dorm. She loved the subject matter and she loved her job, but she knew she would miss Rory's rapt attention and secret smiles, even if sometimes it made her blush to think about what they did outside of class. Overall, however, Rory dropping the class was for the best. It was bad enough her lover invaded her thoughts when she wasn't with her; seeing Rory in class two days a week and trying to pretend she didn't know what Rory's lips felt like as they trailed kisses down her neck and collarbone, and how delicious it was to help Rory out of her clothes or to hear her whisper *You're so beautiful*, would have been torture.

But Rory was the real beauty. She almost felt unworthy of someone so beautiful. Maggie was no fool. She knew both men and women found Rory attractive. She had seen some of her other students give Rory looks of appraisal and she definitely couldn't blame them. She was fully aware that Rory could have her pick, but she had chosen her, and there were times when she wasn't sure why. Rory had noticed her, she was sure of it, before she had noticed Rory. Maggie wondered what it had been that had gotten her attention.

She was a good deal older and nearly a foot shorter than Rory. Her long hair now had more strands of silver than she was comfortable with, she was starting to get wrinkles around her mouth and eyes, and the bags under her eyes were big enough to pack for a two-week vacation, which she was sorely in need of. She appraised herself in the mirror as she stood in her bathroom after her shower. The sad truth was that she wasn't twenty-five anymore. Her boobs looked sad and droopy to her critical eye, her skin was pale from an academic life lived indoors, and her stomach, though flat, was not toned. When Rory looked at her with such tenderness or, as often as not, sexual hunger, none of those flaws mattered. She was beautiful and desirable and she believed it.

She knew she was Rory's first and didn't take that lightly. She didn't want to screw this up. On impulse, she grabbed her phone off the sink and texted, *Just thinking of you. Have a great day.* She smiled as she sent it, imagining Rory doing the same when she read it. When the reply came back a minute later, her smile broadened and she sighed with the weight of emotion.

Thank you, love. I hope you have a great day too and I'll miss seeing you this afternoon.

Me too. Come over tonight?

Tonight and every night if you want.

I don't know if I could handle that. Gotta sleep sometime.

That's what your office hours are for.

Maggie laughed out loud, then remembered she was still standing in the middle of her bathroom naked and that she needed to get to campus for those aforementioned office hours. She resisted the urge to continue the conversation and set her phone back down.

She knew she should just revel in the fact that she had been able to get Rory's attention in the first place. She would be the envy of many of her colleagues if they knew, though she knew she would be treated as a pariah by some of the others. Dating a student, she knew, always would be taboo, regardless of the circumstances. The questions of power and consent were legitimate things to be concerned about; she couldn't argue that point. But neither applied to her relationship with Rory. Not only had Rory consented, but she had been the one to pursue the relationship in the first place.

As she was heading out the door, she couldn't help but wonder what her father, a true academic who had loved all his students as he loved his only child, would have thought. On the one hand, he always wanted her happiness, but on the other, integrity had meant a lot to him. Once in the car, she looked at her silver cross dangling from the rearview mirror, a present from her father, which she would always keep though she wasn't religious, and said, "I do hope you understand. I never forced this on her. And maybe I do love her. Would that be so bad?" She sighed as she put the car in gear and backed out of her driveway.

❖

No sooner had Maggie gotten into her office than the phone on her desk rang. She set her worn leather messenger bag on the floor, then answered. "Dr. Parks."

"Margaret, I've just received an email that tells me the roster for your class has changed."

Maggie sat down with a sigh. "Yes, Charles, I received the same email."

"This comes just a few days after I tell you to watch yourself. And this particular student has been getting excellent grades. Looks a bit suspicious, wouldn't you say?"

"As I recall, Charles, you demanded that I stop seeing her. And as far as looking suspicious, no, it doesn't. Students drop classes for a variety of reasons, you know that."

"You can dance around this all you want, but it doesn't change the fact that you've been lying to me this whole time."

He actually sounded hurt. "Charles, I have not lied to you. I have always answered your questions truthfully."

"Then let me ask one more. Are you sleeping with Aurora Morgan?"

Maggie paused. On the one hand, he had no legal right to even ask that question, but on the other hand, she knew if she evaded the question that would look worse. She wasn't going to lie but she weighed her words carefully. "Over the last few days I have started a relationship based on mutual consent with a young woman who is not my student, who is old enough to make her own decisions, and her name is Aurora Morgan."

"Dammit, Margaret! I don't believe you! You're on your own with this. You won't get any support from me or this office. When the shit hits the fan, and believe me, it will, it won't be flying in my direction, I can tell you that." With that, he slammed the phone down.

"Because you've been so supportive up till now," she said to the dial tone, before she replaced the receiver in its cradle. It was starting; she just hadn't thought it would start so soon.

She texted Rory, *I wish you were here right now.*
I always wish that. You okay?
Sigh. Charles.

I'll be in your office in ten.

Wait! As much as I want you here, I don't think now is the best time.

Pause.

Okay. I understand.

Talking with Rory always made her smile. She had to wonder though, what else they had ahead of them. It just seemed ridiculous to her that in this day and age, anyone would care what two consenting adults did, regardless of how they met or their sexual orientation.

Maggie worried a little about how Rory's parents would react, though she had insisted that she was out to them and they'd be fine.

They'd had this discussion on Sunday. They had been sitting at Maggie's small dining room table, enjoying a fabulous pasta dish that Rory had made. Between bites Rory said, "Baby, you're not that much older than me."

"Oh no?"

"No."

"Tell me, how old is your mother?"

Rory laughed. "Relax. She's fifty-one." Rory put her free hand on Maggie's arm. "This is not a Freudian thing. I'm not looking for a mother—I already have a great one. One who's so awesome that she's not going to be alarmed at your age." Maggie gave her a weak smile. Rory removed her hand to grab her glass of wine. She said into her glass, "She's going to be more upset over the religious thing."

"What?"

Rory set her glass down and shrugged. "She's Catholic. She wants me to marry a nice Catholic girl. If you think about it, that's still a progressive attitude, considering how the church feels about homosexuality."

"Yes, but I'm not a nice Catholic girl. Now I have something else to worry about."

Rory had put her fork down and taken Maggie's hand in both of hers. "Yes, she'll probably ask about your religion— that's just what Catholic mothers do, I've noticed—but then she'll be more interested in getting to know you."

"And your father? How's he going to feel about me being with his little girl?"

Rory had waved her hand dismissively. "Don't worry about him, he's a pushover."

Maggie doubted that, but she'd said no more on the subject. It didn't escape her notice that they were skirting around the issue of the future. Part of her felt ridiculous for being such a lesbian cliché. Another part, though, the part of her heart that she hadn't paid much attention to in quite some time, knew that this thing with Rory wasn't a fling and she was already willing to fight for it if it came to that.

CHAPTER ELEVEN

Rory spent Monday night with Maggie but slept in her own bed the rest of the week. Rehearsals were going well. It was going to be a great production, even with Miranda in it. Surprisingly, Miranda seemed to be ignoring her, and she wondered briefly about that, until Rachel's friend Lori showed up after practice Friday night, and she and Miranda kissed in greeting, then left together. Good. Maybe if she had her own relationship, she'd keep her nose out of Rory's.

Though she had dropped Maggie's class, they were still keeping their relationship on the down low, and as a consequence, hardly talked to each other at rehearsal—not unless it was related to the play. But tonight was a big night. Some of Maggie's friends had invited them for drinks after rehearsal, and she was going to meet Maggie there. Now it was Rory's turn to worry.

To her relief, she liked Bill and Dix immediately and Bill put her at her ease as soon as she walked in. "Oh my gosh, Margaret, you didn't tell me you were dating a butched-up Disney princess."

Maggie and Rory both laughed.

"Not so—I'm Irish, not Scottish."

Dix came in from the kitchen and handed Maggie a glass of wine and kissed her on the cheek. "And with sass—I approve." He nodded to Rory with a small smile. "What can I get you to drink, love?"

"Same as Maggie, thanks." Everyone else settled in the living room while Dix got Rory a glass of wine.

"Rory, why haven't I had a class with you yet?"

"Well, it's my first grad semester. What do you teach?"

Before Bill could answer, Dix came in with her glass, handed it to her, and then took his seat next to Bill on the couch, leaving Rory and Maggie to sit close on the love seat.

"Why, costume design, of course."

Dix patted Bill's knee with affection. "Yes, my hubby is such a queer cliché."

"Well, I'm sorry, we can't all teach about ancient dead people."

Maggie turned to Rory. "Dix teaches in the history department."

"It's not all pyramids and war, you know? I also teach a modern queer history class."

"Really? That sounds awesome. When do you teach that?"

"Every fall. This semester we're focusing on World War II. I think next fall it'll be time to do the Stonewall era again."

"Cool. Maybe I'll audit if my schedule's not too tight."

"So, what's your concentration, Rory?" Bill asked.

"Well, currently it's acting but I've been thinking of switching to directing."

"You have?" Maggie sounded surprised.

Rory turned to her. "Yeah, I love acting, but I want to be behind the scenes more, I think."

"What brought this on?"

Rory wasn't sure, but she thought she denoted a note of panic in Maggie's voice. She smiled. "Watching you. You bring such a passion to it—I want that feeling."

Bill and Dix exchanged a smile.

"Well, honey, I'm flattered. If this is what you really want, I say go for it. But, for the record, you're an amazing actress." She turned to Bill and Dix. "You saw *Rent* last year, remember?"

"Oh my God, I thought you looked familiar! You were Maureen, weren't you? You were wonderful," Bill gushed.

"Thanks."

"Oh, and that voice!" Dix chimed in. "So beautiful. You know, I never really liked Maureen, always thought she was such a self-centered bitch, but you made her likeable."

Rory's cheeks were getting hotter and she knew she was blushing. She hoped they would think it was just the wine.

"Maureen is not a bitch. She's just an independent woman who doesn't want to live with restrictions. Nothing wrong with that," Bill said.

"No, there wouldn't be, if she was in an open relationship, but she's not. She's just a cheater. No excuse for that."

"Look at when the play is set—open relationships weren't even a thing back then," Bill interjected.

"You act as if it was forever ago, when it was just set in the nineties," Dix countered.

Maggie noted, "You two do realize you're talking about the morals of a fictional character, right?"

Bill and Dix stopped talking and turned to Maggie in unison. Bill spoke. "Fictional character? That's like saying *Rent* is just some play." Bill snorted. "Please, don't get me started."

Dix stood up to get the bottle of wine from the kitchen. "Please, don't get him started."

"Thank you, sweetie," Bill said to Dix when he refilled his glass, then he leaned forward toward Maggie. "In any event, *Rent*'s depiction of queer characters is light years ahead of your friend Tennessee Williams's plays. The biggest thing he did for gay people was to tell us to stay in the closet. None of his characters were happy."

Rory wasn't sure she should argue with a professor, but hell, she was here as a friend, right? "His writing was indicative of the time he was writing. Besides, it wasn't just gay men who are miserable in his plays—it's women and straight men too. True, he focused on tragic characters, but I always thought he was trying to say something important." Rory leaned forward, getting engrossed in the discussion.

"Yeah, that life sucks for everyone. Things aren't always peachy, but we aren't all miserable and full of self-loathing either."

"Exactly! If you think about it, maybe he could have really been trying to tell straight audiences that gay people weren't so different from them. We all have struggles to overcome. So stop trying to separate us and turn us into the other, when we're not. Our struggles are different, but there're still obstacles we have to get around, same as them."

Maggie put her hand on Rory's knee and leaned over to give her an enthusiastic kiss on the cheek. Dix smiled and nodded. Bill looked thoughtful. "That's a very good point and one I hadn't considered. I may have to reevaluate my stance against the ol' boy."

"Oh my God, Merida, you have done the impossible!" Dix slapped his thigh in enthusiasm.

Instead of being annoyed at Dix as she was when Rachel called her that name, she smiled at him, amused. "Just stating my opinion." She shrugged and sat back on the couch and put her arm around Maggie's shoulders.

"Maggie, I think you have finally met a worthy companion. So much better than Maxine," Bill enthused.

"Who's Maxine?"

Dix nearly spit out his wine. Bill smacked him on the leg.

Maggie sighed. "She was my ex. We broke up two years ago. Can I tell you about her at home?"

Rory gave her a small smile. "Okay. No worries." She kissed Maggie on the forehead.

"Well, that wasn't tense or anything," Dix said as he topped off their glasses.

Everyone laughed.

❖

"I really like Bill and Dix. Thank you for introducing me to them."

Maggie smiled and glanced at Rory as she drove them home. "I'm glad. They seemed to like you too. I'm surprised you let Dix call you Merida."

"I kinda was too. Usually when Rachel does it, it pisses me off. Probably because I know she does it to get on my nerves, and he wasn't."

"Maybe so. I think having butched-up princesses is something Disney should consider, however." Maggie chuckled and patted Rory on the knee.

Rory rested her hand on Maggie's right thigh and let it stay there. Maggie liked the possessive feel.

Then the laughter died away and Rory turned serious. "Hey, Maggie?"

"Yes?"

"Can we invite Rachel over tomorrow night? I want to share this with her. She's my best friend and it feels wrong to keep it from her."

Maggie hesitated. "I just worry because she's still a student. What if she said something to her other friends?"

"She wouldn't do anything that would hurt me."

She sighed. "Okay. I suppose it's only fair. And if we're going to be a part of each other's lives that means all the other people in our lives that come with us."

"I'm glad you feel that way, because my parents are coming down next weekend."

"What?"

Rory laughed. "That was easy."

"You're joking?"

"Yes."

"I swear to God, Aurora Morgan, if I wasn't driving right now…"

"What're you going to do?"

"Just wait until I get you home." She put her hand on top of Rory's and laced their fingers together.

"Promises, promises. Besides, you were going to tell me about Maxine."

Might as well get that over with. Maggie pulled into her driveway and said, "That's right."

Rory squeezed her hand once the car was in park. "It's okay. I know it's your past, and I'm not going to hold it against you. I just want to know. Then I can tell you about my not-so-exciting dating life."

"You're right." Maggie leaned in and gave Rory a soft kiss on the lips. "Okay, let's go do this, because if I don't get to spend the rest of the evening kissing you, I just might die of hunger."

"We wouldn't want that." Rory kissed her but pulled back at the last moment with a chuckle. "You want these lips, baby, you gotta earn them. Come on." She opened her car door and Maggie moaned.

"You are so cruel."

Rory laughed as she went up to the door ahead of Maggie and waited for her to come and unlock it. Maggie followed behind, shaking her head in amusement. She just hoped the good mood would continue as they broached the subject of Maxine. She unlocked the door and they went inside. As Maggie closed the door behind them, Rory grabbed her hand and gave her a small smile, which she returned.

"Come on, let's sit down and you can tell me a story."

Maggie let herself be led to the couch and they sat facing each other. "Okay. God, where to start?"

"At the beginning. How'd you meet?"

"We met when I came to work here six years ago. She taught playwriting, so we ran into each other all the time. When she asked me out it seemed like the most natural thing. We'd had conversations in the past, and I knew we had a lot in common and even had the same views on many things. She was easy to talk to and attractive." Maggie trailed off, not sure how much she should say about that.

Rory didn't seem fazed. "What'd she look like?"

"You really want to know?"

"Yes."

"She was tall, long blond hair, athletic. More a tomboy than anything else."

"So, you have a type?" Rory smirked.

Maggie laughed. "I guess I do."

"I'm sorry, go on."

"Well, we went out, had a good time. After about six months she moved in. We got along well and our lives fit together pretty well. Then about three and a half years later, she told me she wanted to pursue her writing full-time. She had an offer of an Off-Broadway production with an up and coming company run by a lesbian playwright, and Maxine really wanted to work with her, but it would have meant resigning her position and moving to New York. She asked me to go with her, but I was coming up for tenure and I didn't want to just chuck all that." The constant pressure of Rory's hand on her knee and her intent gaze made it easier to continue. "So I told her I would wait here for her while she pursued this dream. She told me I would be waiting forever. She begged me to come and I considered it, I really did. But a little birdie named Bill said something very wise. Why should I have to abandon my dream just so she could follow hers? I realized he was right, but I swear to you, it broke my heart to make that decision. I felt so selfish. And our mutual friends and colleagues mostly blamed me for not supporting her dream."

"Oh, honey, that wasn't selfish. We each have a right to our own dreams and we shouldn't expect someone to give up theirs for ours."

"You are too wonderful for words sometimes, you know that?"

Rory grinned, then cupped Maggie's face gently and slowly drew her to her. "Then no more words."

The kiss Rory gave her was slow and tender and Maggie sighed into it, feeling the tension she had started to feel at Bill and Dix's start to melt away. As she and Rory leisurely kissed on the couch, with one hand entwined in Rory's curls and the other resting on her black leather belt, Maggie vaguely remembered that Rory had said she was going to disclose her relationship history. But as their kisses intensified and Rory's hands found their way under her blouse, she decided the past wasn't important. She let herself be swept up in the moment and only concentrated on Rory.

❖

Saturday morning before rehearsal, Rory texted Rachel. *You got plans tonight?*

IDK. You tell me.

How would you like to meet Maggie?

For reals?

Yes. After rehearsal.

Awesome! Can I give her the third degree?

Ha ha ha. No.

Rory gave her Maggie's address and a time to be there. She was happy that she would no longer have to keep this secret from Rachel. Maggie was very important to her and she wanted to share that with her best friend. Briefly she considered that seeing her and Maggie together might hurt Rachel, but she also knew Rachel accepted that they would never have that kind of relationship and could still be happy for her.

After rehearsal, Rory and Maggie left together, not caring who saw. They didn't leave arm in arm or anything, and as Maggie noted, it wasn't as if they hadn't left together back when they were only going for burgers, so they decided to risk it. No one seemed to pay them any mind.

When Rachel's knock came, Rory ran to the door, tagging Maggie with a high five on the way by, and they exchanged a smile.

Rory opened the door still wearing that smile. "Hey, if it isn't my favorite blonde."

"You say that like you know a lot of blondes and you've rated us all."

"Don't make it weird. Get in here."

"Don't you make it weird." Rachel walked in and took a look around. "So, where is the famous Maggie?"

"She's in the kitchen. I wanted to tell you about her first before I just sprung her on you. Have a seat." She gestured to the couch and Rachel sat, while Rory stayed standing.

"Why are you so nervous? You already told me about the age difference. What more could you be hiding that would surprise me?"

Rory put her hands in her back pockets. "Oh, just one more thing."

"Well, I know my mother doesn't live here, so whoever you're dating can't be all that shocking."

"No, not your mother."

"Out with it already—who's Maggie and what's the big deal?"

"Maggie's full name is…Dr. Margaret Parks."

Rachel's mouth fell open in shock and Rory waited for her full reaction.

Finally, Rachel recovered enough to speak. "Dr. Parks from the theater department?"

"Yeah."

"Shut up! Dr. Parks took your cherry?"

Rory rushed over and put her hand over Rachel's mouth. "For the love of God, stop talking." Rachel's eyes danced and Rory could feel her smile under her hand. Before she could release her, Maggie came out of the kitchen. Rachel's eyes widened as Maggie walked up to Rory and put her hand on Rory's arm.

"Honey, what have I told you about assaulting our guests? You can let her go now." Rory did so with a glare in Rachel's direction. Maggie looked at Rachel. "And for the record, I did not take anything that was not freely given." Maggie took Rory's hand as she regained her composure.

"Sorry, Dr. Parks, I didn't mean any disrespect."

Rory rolled her eyes. "Oh, knock it off, you can be normal."

"Rory's right. You can even call me Maggie if you like." Maggie gave her a warm smile.

"Okay, I'll try."

"Good. Rory, I think the enchiladas are almost done."

"Wonderful. I'll be back." She narrowed her eyes at Rachel. "You play nice."

Rachel put her hand to her chest. "I have no idea what you're talking about."

"I mean it." Rory pointed her finger at Rachel for emphasis.

❖

When Rory was out of the room Rachel sat back down. "So, I wish I could say I've heard a lot about you, but Rory hasn't said much."

"I know. I'm sure you can guess the reason for that." Maggie sat facing Rachel at her desk, much as she had the first time Rory had come by.

"Yeah, I get it. I gotta tell you, I did wonder why Rory wasn't talking."

"Does she normally tell you about her personal life?"

"When she has one. Usually she's holed up in her room, doing her impression of a hermit crab."

Maggie chuckled. "So she doesn't go out much?"

"Not very often, no. I keep telling her she doesn't understand what grad school is really about. She's taking it way too seriously."

"I hope she has *some* fun."

"She does when I can drag her out, which isn't all that often."

"Were you responsible for the glitter?"

Rachel gave a surprised laugh. "Well, I didn't put it on her, if that's what you mean, but she was in my presence when it happened, that's all I'll say."

"I see."

Rachel turned serious. "Were you the reason she was upset that night?"

Maggie sighed and shifted her gaze. "Unintentionally. When I saw her the next day I felt responsible."

Rachel spoke evenly. "You broke her heart that day, you know?"

"I know."

"Don't do it again."

Maggie met Rachel's gaze and held it for many moments. Finally, "I won't, you have my word."

Rachel went quiet, then asked, "You love her?"

"Yes."

Rachel nodded. "Good."

"So do you." It wasn't a question.

Rachel appraised Maggie before she said, "She knows that."

"I'll treat her well, I promise."

"You better." Then Rachel smiled just as Rory came in from the kitchen.

"Dinner's ready."

"Awesome, I can't wait to try it. I didn't know princesses could cook."

"Well, this one can, asshole, let's eat."

"Suddenly feels like there are two teenagers in my house," Maggie said, as she stood up.

Rachel pointed at Rory. "She started it."

"Nuh-uh."

"Enough, both of you. Come on." Maggie took Rory's hand and squeezed it as they headed into the dining room.

❖

Once everyone was seated around the table, Maggie realized she and Rachel shared the common goal of keeping Rory happy. Rachel seemed to mask her feelings for Rory with bawdy humor, but Maggie could see that Rory knew how Rachel felt about her. Rory often gave Rachel soft looks of affection but Maggie wasn't worried. She knew Rory wasn't in love with Rachel, and Rachel knew that too.

"So, how did you two hook up, anyway? Did your eyes meet across a crowded classroom or what?" Rachel asked around a mouthful of Mexican goodness.

Rory and Maggie exchanged a smile, then Rory spoke. "Well, kinda. There was just something about her. I couldn't take my eyes off her." Rory gazed longingly into Maggie's eyes and Maggie smiled back at her.

"Please, I'm eating over here."

Without breaking her gaze with Maggie, Rory said, "Sorry, not sorry."

"My love, we have company."

"She's not company, she's Rachel."

"And she can hear you," Rachel noted.

Rory turned in Rachel's direction. "Oh, are you still here?"

Rachel sneered at her.

"Tell me again—why are you two friends?"

Rory and Rachel exchanged confused looks.

"Because we love each other, right, ho?"

"Absolutely, Merida, without a doubt."

"See?" Rory and Rachel inclined their heads together and gave Maggie innocent smiles.

"Oh, totally. What was I thinking? But, dear, why did you just call her a ho?"

"Oh, because she is one, but I love her anyway."

"My God, you two sound like siblings."

"I told you, Rachel's my sister from another mister."

With the tension eased, they went back to casual conversation, Rory and Rachel teasing each other some more and Maggie and Rory continuing to give each other loving looks or holding hands. Just like the night before with Bill and Dix, this evening felt natural and cozy to Maggie. She could get used to this life.

Chapter Twelve

The more Rory thought about it, the more she wanted to introduce Maggie to her parents. She knew there was no reason to keep their relationship from them. She understood why Maggie was nervous, but she knew her parents and she knew they would not make an issue of things.

She had returned to her room somewhat reluctantly on Sunday evening. Leaving Maggie was becoming more and more difficult. She sighed as she set her bag down. She missed Maggie, it was just that simple. She sat on her bed, pulled out her phone, and sent a quick text.

I just realized I'm missing something.

Oh? Did you leave something here?

Yeah. You.

Aww. You're very sweet. I miss you too.

Rory gave another sigh, then she dialed her mother.

"Well, if isn't my firstborn. How are you, my dear?"

"Still your only child, Mom."

"Yes, but you'll always be my firstborn."

"You're weird."

"And you are my child."

"What are you trying to say?"

"Nothing, my sweetness."

"Uh-huh. Anyway, can we talk like normal now?"

"Yes, because even I can only take so much schlock."

"Exactly." Rory paused a moment, took a deep breath, then went for it. "I want you and Dad to meet someone."

"Oh. Someone special, I assume?"

"Very much."

"I'm listening."

"Her name is Maggie and she's brilliant and beautiful and I…I think I…" Words suddenly failed her.

"You love her?"

Rory exhaled. "I think so, yeah."

"Oh, honey, I'm so happy for you. And your father will be too. So tell me more."

"Okay, but don't freak out."

"Honey, I'm sure I'm not going to freak out. If you love her, I'm sure I will too."

"Oh, I wouldn't be so sure about that."

"Aurora Dawn Morgan, stop dithering and just tell me."

"Okay." She paused again then said very rapidly, "Maggie's my forty-year-old professor. Was, isn't anymore."

"Wait a minute, slow your roll, missy." It sounded as if her mom was angry, something that didn't happen often. Rory knew enough to stop talking. "You're dating your professor?"

"Well, she's not anymore. I mean, I dropped her class."

"You dropped a class for this woman?"

"I can pick up another one, no big deal."

"No big deal? Since when do you treat grad school like it's no big deal?"

"Mom, I thought you would be happy for me…supportive. I always thought you were the cool mom. Hell, even Rachel wants you and Dad to adopt her."

"Don't try to guilt me about this, I have legitimate concerns. And what about Rachel? She's a nice girl—why aren't you dating her? What's wrong with her?"

"Nothing's wrong with her, I just don't think of her like that. She's like my sister."

Her mom sounded calmer when she spoke again. "Just answer me this. Who chased who?"

Rory gave a nervous, somewhat relieved laugh. "Oh, I totally chased her. She didn't pursue me at all, even gave me a whole list of reasons why it wouldn't work."

"Which you ignored, I take it?"

Rory's laugh was more genuine this time. "Which I ignored, right."

"So you used all that charm you inherited from me to convince her to go out with you, to which she said, yes, of course, and things escalated from there?"

"Basically."

"I see. Well, your father and I will definitely have to meet her so we can put our minds to rest about this. Arrange that and get back to me."

"I will. Thanks, Mom."

"Don't thank me yet, little girl."

Rory didn't call Maggie back that night. She hadn't figured out what to say yet. She needed time to think, to figure out how to bring up the subject without scaring Maggie the way she had scared her mother.

Her mother's reaction had surprised her at first, but when she thought about it, it made sense. Would she want to hear a daughter of hers was dating a professor? Absolutely not. A parent's cool had limits, and she had found hers.

Monday morning, when she knew Maggie was in her office, Rory finally had the courage to give her a call.

"Dr. Parks."

"Who's the sexiest looking professor in the theater department?" Rory's voice had a singsong quality to it.

The immediate reply was, "Dr. Baskin, everyone knows that."

Rory could hear the smile in Maggie's voice. "Well, I disagree and I'm part of everyone."

"Yes, but you're biased, so your opinion doesn't count."

"I concede you may have a point there."

"So is this why you called, to take a poll on sexy teachers?"

"Well, a girl's gotta keep her options open."

"Uh-huh."

"Okay, I did have one other reason…"

"I thought so."

"It's nothing bad. I just…I talked to my mother."

Rory heard Maggie inhale and it took her a moment before she responded.

"I wish you had talked to me first. I'm not sure I'm ready to meet them yet, if that's what you had in mind. I mean, meeting your lover's parents is always a big step, without adding our circumstances into it. I just don't know…"

Rory felt deflated. First her mother's short burst of anger, and now Maggie's reluctance. She understood both of them, but it was still disheartening. "I'm sorry for not asking you. I just thought it'd be okay."

Maggie sighed again. "It's okay, it just took me off guard. I guess I just thought I'd have more time to prepare. That our relationship would be more than a few weeks old."

"It'll be okay, I promise. I'll be next to you the whole time, holding your hand."

"You better be, buster, or I'll make sure of it."

Rory laughed, glad Maggie was in better spirits and making jokes. "You have my word."

❖

Saturday evening after rehearsal, they rushed home so Maggie could shower and Rory could cook for her parents, something she always enjoyed doing.

Maggie stared at her open closet door, not at all sure what to wear. Should she wear something conservative, like what she'd wear in the classroom, or something more casual, like jeans? She didn't know, but she knew who would. She grabbed her phone off her bedside table and dialed Bill.

"Hey, sweetie. So tonight's the big night, huh? You nervous? What am I saying? Of course you are, why else would you be calling me?"

Maggie smiled, instantly at ease. "I need help, Bill, I don't know what to wear."

"Something that says, *I promise, I'm not a cougar.*"

"God, I hate that expression."

"I don't know, makes the older woman sound kind of fierce, if you ask me."

"Yeah, like a wild animal. Wild, I am not. They don't have terms like this for men."

"No, the terms for men are worse. If you're a straight man dating a younger woman...Okay, bad example. You're right, it's usually the woman who gets the bad name there."

"Exactly."

"But if you're a gay man you get called a chicken hawk. Now I ask you, which is worse—a chicken hawk or a cougar?"

Maggie laughed. "I don't know. They're both pretty awful. Now, are you going to help me or not?"

"Okay, let me guess. You're currently standing in front of your closet, naked, trying to find the perfect symmetry between boring schoolmarm and evil temptress who lured their daughter into her wicked lesbian lair," Bill said mischievously.

"Your perception of lesbians is a bit worrisome."

"All gay men think lesbians are wicked, but we're not talking about that right now. We need to get you dressed. Okay, here's what you do. Pull out your best dark blue jeans and pair them with your most expensive silk blouse."

Maggie scanned her clothes, found the jeans, and laid them across her bed. "Why does it have to be the most expensive?" she asked, as she searched for the one he referenced, a dark red button-down that looked great when she paired it with a suit, but she had no idea how it looked paired with jeans.

"Because this look says, *I'm casual and relaxed, but make no mistake, I have money in the bank.*"

"I see. That makes perfect sense," she said wryly, as she set the blouse on top of the jeans. She had to admit, they looked good together.

"Are you making fun of me, Miss I-don't-know-how-to-dress-myself?"

Maggie laughed easily. "Not at all, my dear. I do appreciate your help."

"I'm glad. Let me know how it goes."

"You know I will." She hung up and put the phone back on the nightstand, then began to get dressed. Just as she was tucking her shirt in, with her back to the bedroom door, she heard a whistle from behind her and, startled, turned around to see Rory leaning in the doorway, with her arms crossed over her chest. "You scared me."

"And you floor me." Rory gave Maggie her best lascivious smile.

"Are you leering at me?"

"Only with deep respect and admiration, I promise."

"Uh-huh." She turned to fully face Rory, with her arms down at her sides. "How do I look, really?"

Rory slowly walked up to her, her grin becoming a smile, and put her hands on Maggie's shoulders. "I've never seen you more beautiful. And I'm glad you're leaving your hair down. I love seeing it."

Instead of its usual tight braid, Maggie had only tamed her hair with a clip that kept it pulled back in a loose ponytail. Rory loved it but dared not touch it, not yet. She settled, instead, for taking Maggie's face in her hands and putting a gentle kiss on her lips. When Rory pulled away, Maggie was smiling.

"Thank you, my dear. I needed that." She wrapped her arms around Rory's waist, holding on to the back of Rory's belt, and pulled Rory tighter against her. She glanced down at the T-shirt and jeans Rory was wearing, the same clothes she had worn at rehearsal, and asked, "Aren't you going to change?"

"Not really. I have a button-down in the other room I'll put on over this." Maggie smiled and shook her head. "What? You think I should wear something else?"

"No, I'm just amused that for you, getting dressed up means putting on a shirt and you're done."

"Well, it doesn't hurt to look this good." Rory pulled away enough to use her hand to indicate the length of her body, and she grinned at Maggie's shocked face.

Maggie released Rory and gave her a playful shove. "That's it, out of my bedroom!" Maggie pointed to the door but couldn't keep the grin off her face.

Rory smiled back. "Oh, that's a first."

"And it won't be the last, if you don't go now."

Rory backed up toward the door, her hands up in surrender. "I'm going, I'm going." She started to leave, then poked her head back in the door. "Oh, by the way, Mom and Dad will be here in ten minutes"—she glanced at the clock—"or more like five minutes now"—then ducked to dodge the pillow that came flying toward the general vicinity of her head. She quickly left, laughing the whole time.

❖

When Maggie came out of her room a few minutes later, Rory was opening the door to two good-looking people—a tall, beautiful redheaded woman and a tall blond man. They looked just as nervous as she felt. She smiled as she came into the room and two pairs of eyes immediately appraised her; Maggie briefly wondered what they saw. "Mr. and Mrs. Morgan, hello. Welcome. Won't you come in?" Rory smiled at her, came to stand beside her, and took her hand as promised. Mrs. Morgan made note of this, Maggie could tell, but her expression was otherwise unreadable.

"Thank you." Mrs. Morgan came up to Maggie first with her hand outstretched. "Hello, I'm Ann."

Maggie shook the proffered hand. "Margaret—Maggie."

"Nice to meet you, Maggie. I'm John."

"Likewise, John. Everyone come in, have a seat. Would anyone like a glass of wine?"

"Oh, please," Ann said. "I think that we can all use some."

"I'll get it, Mom." Rory squeezed Maggie's hand before she let go and headed into the kitchen. Maggie did her best not to look after her longingly, like a sad pup. Instead, she took a seat at her desk.

"I know you're nervous but don't be," John said. "We're just as afraid of you as you are of us, so…" John smiled and Maggie saw Rory's glint in his eye. That, coupled with his humor, put her at ease.

"Oh, don't be afraid of me, I'm not scary at all."

Ann said, "I think he just means that, well, you're the one who's going to take our daughter away from us."

Maggie shifted uncomfortably. "I see. Well, I'm not trying to take her away from you."

"Oh, we knew someone would come along someday, it was only a matter of time," John said. "And college is definitely a good place to find your soul mate." He looked at his wife and smiled and reached for her hand.

"Yes, that's where we met. I took one look at that smile and his sparkling blue eyes and I thought, he thinks he's all that. I don't want that jerk coming anywhere near me."

Everyone laughed.

"But I grew on you," John said, looking at Ann with clear affection.

"Like mold, dear...eventually." She looked at Maggie. "Rory tells me it took a while for her to charm you as well." At that moment, Rory brought out a tray with four glasses of wine. "Aurora, since when do you drink wine? I thought you couldn't stand it?"

After Rory had given everyone a glass, she sat on the floor next to Maggie's chair and leaned against Maggie's legs. She shrugged. "Maggie has good wine."

Ann looked at Maggie almost conspiratorially. "I never thought I'd see the day when she drank something that didn't come in a brown longneck bottle."

"Well, she's free to bring some over, but I never have it in the house. Never could stand it."

"Me neither." Ann shuddered. "But they bond over one every time she's home."

Rory and John smiled at each other, then John said, "I'll tell you what. I want to get our cards on the table so we can release the tension in here before it pops like an overstuffed balloon. That way we can enjoy the rest of the evening."

Maggie shifted some in her seat and put her hand on Rory's shoulder. Rory pulled her knees up to her chest, wineglass in both hands. She looked into her glass.

"I think your mother and I are mainly concerned about two things. Do you see a future together, and is this relationship going to make life difficult for either of you?"

"Difficult in what way?" Maggie asked.

"Well, your job, for starters. I know that student-teacher relationships are discouraged, for good reason. Even though this is a consensual relationship, when others find out about it they're going to have their own opinions, and most people can't keep their mouths shut. It could get rocky, is what I'm saying." John was on the edge of his seat on the couch, leaning forward.

"We've talked about it, Dad. I think we're prepared."

"I hope so."

"And what about the first question?" Ann asked.

Rory moved aside so that she could look up at Maggie somewhat expectantly. Maggie gave her a warm smile and couldn't help herself from caressing Rory's cheek. Rory closed her eyes at the touch. When Maggie looked at John and Ann Morgan again, she was smiling. "Yes, in answer to your question, I do see a future with Rory." She took a deep breath, brushed a curl out of Rory's eyes, and, without looking at the Morgan's, said, "I love your daughter very much."

Rory's eyes looked glassy as she looked up at Maggie. "You do?"

"Yes. Very much." Rory's parents had gone silent during this exchange.

Rory shifted so she was now totally facing Maggie and took both her hands in hers. "I love you too. I've just been afraid to say it. I thought it was too soon."

Maggie laughed. "It probably is but that doesn't mean it's

not true. I love you, Aurora Morgan, with all my heart." With a big grin on her face, Rory sprang to her feet, pulled Maggie out of her chair, and put her arms around Maggie in a crushing hug.

Rory pulled back enough to give Maggie a brief kiss. "I promise you won't regret this."

Ann walked over to where Maggie and Rory stood in each other's arms. "I'm happy for you, baby." She threw her arms around her daughter, who let go of Maggie to hug her mother.

John went to Maggie with his hand outstretched and a smile on his face. "Well, she's your responsibility now. I guess we're done raising her."

Maggie laughed and shook his hand. "You've done a fine job."

"Are you trying to give me away again?" Rory joked to her father. "First, it was the circus when I was six, now this? Though, I must admit, I like this option better."

John sighed. "It's a father's lot in life to give away his daughter." Then he grinned. "But I was sad to lose the free peanuts the circus offered."

Everyone laughed, then Maggie said, "I'll give you peanuts, John. It's a small price to pay." Maggie put both arms around Rory's waist and hugged her. Rory kissed her on top of her head.

"Will you?" John said in mock relief. "That's all right then. Speaking of peanuts, let's eat."

"I'm supposed to say that," Rory said.

"Then say it, child. I just gave my only child away for peanuts—I need some kind of nourishment."

❖

After Maggie hugged Rory's parents good-bye, Rory had some time alone with her mom.

"Aurora, I really am happy for you, but please, just slow down a bit. You have your whole lives ahead of you. Let things happen in their own time."

"I will, Mom."

"And, not that you need it, but you have my blessing."

Rory smiled and put her arms around her mother again. "Thanks, Mom."

John came up behind Rory and put his hands on her shoulders. "All right, break it up. Your mother and I have to go home and cry about how our baby's not a little girl anymore." He leaned down and kissed her on the cheek. "Love you, Aurora."

"Love you too, Dad." Maggie came and put one arm around Rory's waist and Rory put her arm across Maggie's shoulders. They stood in the doorway waving, arm in arm, with smiles on their faces, waving as Rory's parents drove off. Maggie put her head on Rory's shoulder and Rory kissed her on top of her head.

"So, how'd I do?"

"Oh, my love, you were wonderful. But I had no doubt that you would be." They headed back inside once Rory's parents were gone from sight. Maggie started to walk ahead toward the bedroom, when Rory reached out to grab her hand. "Now you're just going to walk away?"

"I'm sorry, I'm so worn out that social courtesy is apparently beyond me right now. I was just going to go change." Maggie gestured vaguely behind her and tried to tug Rory along but Rory just grinned at her and quickly pulled Maggie to her. Maggie screamed in surprised delight.

"Not yet, you're not. You think I'm gonna let the woman I love out of my sight that quickly?" She shook her head. "I don't think so." Rory crushed Maggie to her and gave her such a passionate kiss, Maggie seemed to forget just how worn-out she was. She threw her arms around Rory's neck, grabbed handfuls of Rory's curls, and moaned in pleasure. Finally, after several moments, Maggie pulled away for air. She stayed in Rory's embrace and smiled at her.

"So, where did all this passion come from?" Maggie asked.

"From you, my love."

"From me?"

"Yes. Oh, my love, you make me feel as if I have finally become real, and I know I will always be real now."

"I'm glad. I'm also glad I haven't loved all your fur off." Maggie playfully tugged on Rory's hair and Rory laughed.

"That reminds me, been wondering if I should get my hair cut. What do you think? Maybe chopping it to just above my ears and having it shaved in the back. I think that would be cool, right? Or a fifties greaser look, with the sides slicked back and a curl askew on my forehead." Rory gave Maggie a serious look but she could only sustain it for a moment, as Maggie was giving her such a horrified expression.

"Aurora Dawn Morgan, you touch one curl on this head and I'll yank it out myself."

"That doesn't make any sense."

"It does because I say it does."

"Uh-huh. What about you?" Rory began to run her fingers through Maggie's hair.

"Don't worry, mine's not going anywhere either."

"Are you sure about that?" Before Maggie could question her further, Rory kissed her again, this time reaching up to unfasten the clip that held Maggie's waist-length hair back, threw the clip aside, and let the hair fall. Maggie leaned her head back and Rory trailed kisses down her throat. Between kisses, Rory murmured, "So beautiful...you're so beautiful. I love you so much." Rory tugged Maggie's shirt out of her jeans, then began to unbutton it. She trailed her lips down Maggie's chest and pushed the blouse off her shoulders, letting it fall to the floor. Rory dropped to her knees, wrapping her arms around Maggie's waist, and began to kiss down her body. She reached up to undo the buttons on Maggie's jeans.

"Wait."

Rory stopped her ministrations, with one hand on Maggie's fly and the other cupping Maggie's denim-clad ass. She looked up questioningly. "What's the matter? You want me to stop?"

Maggie hesitated then gave Rory such a loving smile. She put both hands on Rory's shoulders. "I just want to slow down, is all. We have all night, my love. Come here."

Rory stood up, feeling as if she had just been knighted. "Yes, my love. What can I do for my lady fair?"

Maggie giggled. "Take me to my bedchamber and make slow, sensual love to me until I am sated."

Rory put one arm behind her back, took Maggie's hand and kissed it, then bowed with a flourish. "As the lady wishes." Then, before Maggie knew what was happening, Rory had picked her up and proceeded to carry her as if she was carrying a bride over the threshold. Maggie squealed and grabbed Rory around the neck.

With fear and laughter in her voice, Maggie said, "Dear God, I never realized how tall you are."

"Don't be afraid. I got you."

"I know that, I trust you."

Rory walked the short distance to Maggie's room, gently put her on the bed, then crawled in next to her and proceeded to do as her lady bade.

Chapter Thirteen

Waking up the morning after having sex for the first time had been energizing, but Rory'd had no idea she would feel so alive the morning after finding out that Maggie loved her. She hadn't meant to get so carried away the night before but she had just been so excited. She wanted to spend all of her time letting Maggie know how much she meant to her. On Sunday morning Maggie still lay sleeping on her side of the bed, not stirring when Rory put her arm around her waist nor when she kissed her naked shoulder. Instead, she curled up with her pillow and rolled closer to the edge of the bed. Rory chuckled and decided to get out of bed. She found her shirt at the foot of the bed, then went to her backpack on the floor by the closet and pulled out a clean pair of boxers. She really had to ask Maggie for drawer space. Once clad, she padded out of the room to the kitchen with breakfast on her mind.

The only reason there currently were staples like bacon and eggs in Maggie's fridge was because Rory insisted she have them. Maggie hadn't been much for eating breakfast before Rory came along, preferring nothing but strong coffee until lunch, when she would likely as not go for a sandwich and salad at the student union food court. Since Rory spent more nights in Maggie's house than she did in the dorm, Maggie now had breakfast nearly every morning and a lunch packed with leftovers from the night before.

Rory loved cooking for people, but for Maggie especially. It was one small way she could show her how much she loved her. Her mother was right—they had the rest of their lives to figure it all out, just sit back and enjoy the ride. Suddenly unable to keep her joy inside, Rory started to sing a John Lee Hooker song softly to herself and jumped at Maggie's voice.

"Good morning, my love," Maggie said with a smile. She came into the room wearing nothing but a dark blue men's pajama top and gave Rory a quick kiss. "What did I ever do to deserve to have such a hot, sexy, young thing like you make me breakfast in your boxers?" Maggie gave Rory's ass a small pat as she passed her to get to the coffeepot.

"Hey, if you're going to keep feeling up the help, I'm gonna have to file a complaint with HR."

Maggie added sugar to her cup and looked thoughtful. "Can't afford another write-up."

"Exactly. You don't want me to have to take disciplinary action, do you?" Rory stressed the word *disciplinary.*

Maggie grinned but said nothing.

"I'm not sure what that grin means."

Maggie threw her head back and laughed. "Good. Keeps you guessing." She turned from the counter and leaned against it. "So, what's for breakfast?"

"You, my love, are about to dine on French toast and bacon. Eggs too, if you want. Do you want?"

"Mm, it all sounds wonderful. Yes, eggs too, please."

"Coming right up." Rory cracked an egg into the skillet.

Maggie kept her place at the counter and continued to watch Rory work. Rory could feel her eyes on her but she relaxed. She knew they were loving eyes that just liked what they saw. That thought made her smile.

"Too bad you're not making scrambled eggs," Maggie said.

Rory turned around. "Oh, did you want scrambled? I should have asked, sorry."

"No, I don't. I just wanted to watch you make them."

"Why? Oh." Rory grinned and wagged a finger at her. "Naughty girl."

Maggie shrugged. "Hey, I like what I see. Is that a problem?"

"Uh-huh. Well, I'm not on the menu...right now."

"Pity." They exchanged a grin.

"I see someone woke up on the horny side of the bed this morning. Apparently, I didn't fulfill my mission last night." Rory grabbed a plate off the counter next to her and started to fill it with sweet and savory goodness.

"Oh, you did fine. Can't a girl want more of a good thing?" Maggie took the plate she was offered, giving Rory a nice slow kiss in the process.

"What have I done? You're insatiable."

Maggie laughed wickedly. "Yep, totally your fault too. Meet you in the dining room." Maggie let her hand linger on Rory's arm a moment, then she walked out of the room.

Rory followed close behind with her own plate and coffee and took a seat at the table.

"I know this is going to sound random, but I just keep going back to your parents' visit last night. They're wonderful people. I'm just glad I won their approval."

"I knew they would love you. Just as I knew you'd make a great first impression."

"Well, I'm glad you were confident—one of us needed to be."

"You had nothing to worry about."

"Easy for you to say. You weren't the one with so much

to prove. As the older woman, coming from such a position of authority, the ball was in my court to prove my worth." Rory suddenly sat her fork down, amusement now gone from her face. In its place was something Maggie couldn't read. She put her own fork down and reached for Rory's hand, but Rory pulled her hand away. "Baby, what's wrong?"

Barely audible, she said, "Don't call me that."

Confused, Maggie said, "Okay, if you don't like it, I won't. Are you okay?"

"I think I'm going to be sick." Rory pushed her chair away from the table and quickly went back into the kitchen. Maggie went after her, concerned.

"Rory?" Rory was standing at the sink with her back to the door, hands on the edge in a death grip, and her head was down. Maggie went to her and put her hand on Rory's back but Rory shrugged her off. "Are you mad at me for something?"

Rory sniffed and wiped her eyes but said nothing.

"Honey, why are you crying? I won't know unless you talk to me." Rory moved away from the sink as Maggie tried to get closer to her again. Instead, Rory stood in the middle of the room, hugging her arms to her chest and looking at Maggie with such anguish, Maggie's heart felt like it was breaking just watching her. Maggie stayed where she was, though it hurt her not to reach out to Rory. "Did I say something wrong? Please tell me, so I can fix this. Whatever it is, whatever you're thinking, I love you."

"No, you don't. You just said that so my parents would like you. You said it yourself, the burden of proof was on you. But it was all a lie, wasn't it? You said whatever you had to say so that my parents wouldn't get pissed that their daughter was dating her old professor. And they bought it. And so did I."

Tears were streaming down Maggie's face as she realized why Rory was so upset. "No! I do love you, I swear! The burden of proof thing, I just meant"—words started to fail her as she tried to explain—"I just meant that I was the one under scrutiny, so I had a right to be nervous. But that doesn't mean I lied."

"Bullshit. I don't believe you."

"What do you want me to say? This is a misunderstanding, that's all."

"A misunderstanding? I'm outta here."

Rory turned to leave but, desperate, Maggie grabbed her by the arm.

"Let go."

"Rory, just listen to me…"

"Please, let me go."

Maggie put her hand on Rory's face. Rory didn't turn away. "Rory, if you walk out that door…If you walk out that door…"

"What, you're done? We're over?"

"No. If you walk out that door, do you know how completely empty I'd be if you were gone? You've been in my heart longer than I even knew and now that you know that too, I want you to settle there. I just love you so much." She gathered Rory in a hug. For a long, agonizing moment, Rory just stood there, not moving. Maggie kissed her neck and whispered, "Please don't go. Oh God, please don't go. Please don't go. I love you so much."

Slowly, Rory's arms went around Maggie and she crushed Maggie to her. She was shaking with sobs. Her tears fell on Maggie's shirt. Maggie absorbed the tears, feeling them seep through to her skin, where she had a feeling she would always feel them as a reminder of the day she very nearly broke Rory's heart for real and came close to losing her. She never wanted to forget that. She whispered, "It's okay, I've got you."

Rory sniffed then replied, "I know that. I trust you."

❖

They went back to bed instead of getting dressed, but not for sex. Maggie wanted to spend the day proving to Rory how much she loved her. There were a lot of quiet moments when no words were needed and Maggie just held Rory to her heart, her arms around her, her hand lazily stroking Rory's hair.

Maggie was propped up with Rory lying with her head in Maggie's lap, when Rory said, "Tell me about your parents. You don't talk about them."

"My parents? What about them?"

Rory turned on her back and smiled up at Maggie. "Anything you want. Will they like me?"

Maggie laughed. "Oh, my love, anyone who doesn't like you, I don't want to be their friend." Maggie slipped a pillow under Rory's head.

"Thank you. And stop deflecting."

"Okay." Maggie exhaled. "The truth is, my father died a few months after Maxine left. He had been slowly dying for years, but that last year he went downhill fast."

"Oh, honey." Rory took Maggie's hand. "What was wrong with him?"

"Cirrhosis. He had had a drinking problem for years, but when I came along my mother told him that she wasn't going to raise her child around an alcoholic, and he better shape up or ship out."

"Good for her."

"Yes. And it worked. He stopped drinking, became a devoted husband and father from that day forward. And he was a great father. I was his little buddy. He took me everywhere, hence my taste in music." Rory smiled up at her. "But by then the damage had already been done. We just wouldn't find out until years later. By the time he passed, Maxine had been living in New York for a few months and I was still grieving the end of that relationship. If not for Bill and Dix…well, they really came through for me."

"I'm glad you had them, at least. What about your mother? I mean, I know she had just lost her husband, but was she not there for you?"

"My mother hasn't been there for me since I came out. She only talks to me now when she feels she has to, like Dad's death, my birthday, and Christmas. And when she does, she never asks me anything about my personal life. That part of my life doesn't exist for her. The calls are just perfunctory." She shrugged indifferently. "So, my love, I doubt she will ever even want to know you exist, let alone meet you. I'm sorry, because you're definitely worth it." Maggie smiled as she brushed Rory's hair back.

Rory sat up and faced Maggie, and gave her a soft kiss on the lips. "You and I are a family now."

Maggie smiled and brushed her fingers against Rory's cheek. "Yes, my love, we are."

❖

Monday mornings were always difficult but this one was especially painful. Maggie hated that Rory had to leave her.

They stood in the living room, Maggie about to walk out the door, Rory there to give Maggie her thermos of coffee. Maggie took the thermos and gave Rory a light kiss. "Thank you, my love." Then she placed it in a side pocket in her messenger bag. "You don't have any classes today, right?"

"Not anymore, nope."

"Well, if you want, you can hang out here." Maggie smiled, suddenly shy.

Rory put her arms around Maggie's waist and grinned. "Are you trying to keep me prisoner? Not that I mind, I just want to clarify so I can plan accordingly. I might have to cancel some things."

"Well, you know, it's not easy for a woman my age to find a stud like you, so that might be something I have to consider."

"You think I'm a stud?"

"Oh yeah. A hot, sexy, butch stud. You weren't aware?"

"No. I mean, I suspected, but that's not the same as knowing."

"Well, now you know." They laughed together and Rory gave Maggie a more meaningful kiss good-bye.

"I will miss you today."

"I'll miss you too, but alas, I cannot spend the whole day here. I have to obtain fresh, uh, clothes."

Maggie laughed. "You mean boxers?"

"Well, those are clothes, yes." Rory was blushing and it made Maggie giggle.

"Considering what we do in there"—Maggie pointed to her bedroom—"I can't believe the mere mention of your undergarments makes you blush."

"Hey, they're called unmentionables for a reason, you know?"

Still laughing, Maggie said, "Come on, stud, I'll drop you off at your dorm."

"Okay. I'll swap clothes and do some homework, then come over this evening."

"Good. You better."

"You're getting bossy and demanding."

"See, this is what happens when you date your teacher. Now move your ass, we have to go."

"Yes, ma'am, I'm coming." Rory picked up her backpack, slid it on one shoulder, and followed Maggie out.

❖

When her grumbling stomach reminded Maggie to eat, she decided to take her lunch outside and enjoy the late fall weather before it became too cold to do so. She picked up her bag and her thermos and headed out the door. Her destination was the lake, a bench near the spot she and Rory had stopped to enjoy the sunset together. Maggie hoped to sit and enjoy her lunch without distractions. She had even left her phone on her desk. Instead, she was content to just soak up nature, enjoy the meal that had been packed with love, and let her thoughts wander.

Her thoughts didn't get a chance to wander for long, however, when a shadow fell over the bench and Maggie looked to her left to see Bonnie, one of her colleagues, standing there, smiling.

"Well, looks like you found a perfect spot. Mind if I join you?"

"Oh, please. I have no claims on the bench. Come and enjoy the sunshine." Maggie patted the spot next to her.

"Thank you. Beautiful day."

"Very much."

"I don't get out to enjoy it often enough. I get so into what I'm doing, I lose track of time and before I know it, the day's gone."

"I know what you mean. I've often thought they should serve us vitamin supplements instead of pastries at our department meetings to make up for all the sun we're not getting." They shared a laugh.

"That would definitely help. Though I have to admit, the Danishes are good. Would hate to lose those."

"That's a good point." On impulse, Maggie reached into

her bag and pulled out the cupcake Rory had packed. A note came out too, but she thought nothing of it. She offered the treat to her colleague. "Well, I don't have a Danish, but would you like a cupcake?"

The woman smiled delightedly. "You know, I haven't had one of these in a long while. Are you sure you don't want it?"

"No, go ahead."

"Well, thank you." The woman glanced down as she took the proffered snack and Maggie could tell that her eyes fell on the note, which Rory had signed simply, *R*.

Instead of trying to hide the note, Maggie ignored it. "Enjoy. They're just too sweet for me."

"Oh, not me. I've always loved them." There was silence between them while Bonnie unwrapped her prize and took a bite. "I wish my husband packed my lunch. That'd be a nice change of pace." Maggie said nothing, just gave her a polite smile. "Of course, I know you don't have a husband but someone obviously was nice enough to pack your lunch."

"Yes, someone was. Definitely a nice gesture."

After a moment, Bonnie said, "I haven't really talked to you about Maxine. I know it's been a while, but I just wanted to say I was sorry how that all turned out."

"So was I. But it's over and done with now. Life goes on." Maggie shrugged.

"Yes. You have moved on, haven't you?" Bonnie asked cautiously.

Maggie waited a beat before she responded, then spoke levelly when she did. "Yes, I have. It's been years since she left. I wasn't going to pine away forever." Maggie gave a chuckle she really didn't feel, but she was trying to keep things light.

"So, what's it like dating someone so much younger?"

"What are you talking about?"

"What am I talking about? Everyone knows, Margaret.

You know secrets like yours don't get kept for very long. Especially around here."

"What exactly does everyone know?"

"We all know about Ms. Morgan. And I have to tell you, people have already started choosing sides."

"What is it, a slow news day?" Maggie couldn't keep the anger out of her voice, though she tried to calm down.

"You know anytime something like this happens, it spreads like wildfire and everyone's suddenly abuzz."

"Something like what, exactly?"

"You know…when a teacher dates a student."

"Ms. Morgan is no longer my student."

"Yes, but she's still a student in this department and it's a small department."

"I see. I guess small minds will talk about small topics."

Bonnie looked hurt. "It's human nature, I think."

"Well, it's an ugly aspect of it. If you'll excuse me, I have to go prepare for class." Maggie quickly packed up her lunch bag and stood up to go. Bonnie put her hand on Maggie's arm to stop her. Maggie tried not to show her disgust. She had never had a problem with Bonnie before, but now found her part of a petty horde of idiots.

"For the record, I'm all for it. You're not doing anything wrong at all. I approve." Bonnie smiled.

Maggie looked at her, incredulous. She couldn't stop herself from saying, "Congratulations, you want a cookie?"

"I was just trying to say I'm on your side."

"There is no side to be on. This is my life, my decision, and quite frankly, my business." She turned to leave then looked at Bonnie again. "And you can tell the rest of the idiot horde that I don't care what side they're on. They won't change any decisions I make from here on out. I have never needed nor sought their approval. And for those who disagree, they can kiss my ass." With that, her final word on the subject, Maggie stalked off.

Bonnie called after her. "Someday, you'll regret alienating everyone. I was just trying to be your friend."

Maggie said nothing and kept walking.

Chapter Fourteen

As opening night for *Cat on a Hot Tin Roof* approached, the atmosphere in the theater was amping up to match the emotionally charged scenes they were rehearsing. Maggie chose to give the cast extra downtime in an effort not to fray their nerves too much.

Rory was sitting with her eyes closed in her favorite seat in the front row on the aisle, across from Maggie and Arenda. Her legs were stretched out in front of her, her arms folded in her lap, her head back on the seat. She might have been sleeping or meditating, but she was doing neither. She was listening to all the sounds in the room. There were several conversations going on at once, each coming from a different part of the room, each voice at a different level. On top of the voices was the sound of footsteps, both on carpet and across the wooden stage. Someone in the row behind her had earbuds in, but their volume was up loud. Rory couldn't detect the words, but she heard the muffled music. She thought of this as theater-zoning, something she only did while in the theater. Not that there was anything wrong with listening to the rest of the world, but she really felt at home in the theater. From the smell of the musty carpet, to the creak of the boards as the actors moved across the stage, to the feeling in the pit of her stomach when the house lights went down, she loved it all.

There was always a pause, a small one that barely registered as taking any time at all, before the stage lights came up. She had always found that time in between to be truly magical. In the small fraction of time, she was transported from the real world to the writer's imaginary one. And the illusion of having gone from one reality to the next lasted as long as the lights were out. But once the house lights came on again, the spell was broken. That part always made her a little sad. It almost felt rude.

"Baby girl, you better wake up." Davis's voice drew her from the zone. "I think Dr. Short Stuff is about to call us to order."

She opened her eyes and smiled at him. "Hello, husband mine."

"Hello, sweetums." Davis grinned at her.

"Since when do you call Maggie Dr. Short Stuff?"

"Since when do you call her Maggie?"

Rory eyed him for a moment, cocked an eyebrow at him, then gave a brief nod. "Touché."

"Touché my ass. You are aware the rumor mill is abuzz about you two?"

"And I'm sure you're aware I don't give a damn."

"Oh, quite. And I don't blame you. Who was it who said, Fuck 'em if they can't take a joke?"

"I don't know, but what in the gay hell are you talking about?"

"What I'm trying to say is people are going to say what they say, especially before they take the time to think about it or who they could be hurting. Which means they're going to end up saying stupid shit, but you just can't let it get to you."

"Okay, but how does that relate to what you quoted?"

"Who cares what other people think about what you do? You don't make decisions about your life based on what they think. Sometimes, the joke is only for your benefit. If they get it, great, if not, fuck 'em."

Rory gave him a confused look for a moment. "That made absolutely no sense, yet, in another way, it made perfect sense. You are very wise, husband mine."

"And you're a sneaky-ass, teacher-loving dyke, but I wouldn't want anyone else for a wife."

Rory laughed and kissed him on the cheek. "Thank you for the convoluted wisdom, homo."

"Ooh, burn."

They were laughing together, when Maggie stood to call everyone to order.

"All right, break over. Let's hit the boards, people." She caught Rory's eye and smiled warmly. Rory had no choice but to return it. Then she leaned over to Davis and whispered, "Just so you know, this is no joke."

Davis gave her such a warm smile in return, Rory couldn't help but give him a brief hug. Davis's acceptance was far better than anyone's approval, as approval made it seem as if she and Maggie had to ask permission. Acceptance just meant an acknowledgment of the truth of something that was meant to be.

Maggie was so intently focused on what was happening on the stage that she didn't hear anyone come into the theater until she felt a presence looming over her, and she looked up to see Charles standing in the aisle, hands in his pockets, looking at the stage.

Maggie said softly, "Charles, you startled me."

"Sorry about that. Can we talk?"

Maggie hesitated, then leaned over to whisper to Arenda,

who promptly gathered her things and moved a few rows back. Maggie then turned back to Charles. "Yes, but you're going to have to talk softer."

Charles just grunted as he made his way to the seat vacated by Arenda. It took him a moment to adjust his six-four frame into the confined space. Maggie covered her mouth with her hand to try to suppress her smile, but he saw it. "Sure, laugh at me all you want. You don't have this problem."

"No, no I don't." When he finally seemed settled, Maggie asked, "So, what brings you down here?"

"Well, it's been a few weeks since I've seen you, just wanted to check in and see how things were going."

"Hmm. I see. Rehearsals are going well. We open the week before Thanksgiving, you know?"

"I do. Glad it's coming together. But it seems so fast."

"I did accelerate the production this year by a few weeks. I've found in the past people had trouble balancing the play with final papers and exams."

"Probably a good thing in the long run then."

"I hope so." They both fell into silence, while Charles pretended to watch the stage and Maggie watched Charles. Finally, Maggie had to ask, "What did you really want to talk about, Charles?"

Charles finally turned in Maggie's direction. "Oh, well, just wanted to check in."

"Bullshit. You want to know if we're still dating, don't you?"

"According to what I've been hearing, I think I already know the answer to that."

"And according to what I've heard, you have a furry fetish. You want to talk about that?" It was an old rumor that had started years ago. Maggie wasn't sure how, nor did she care.

Charles reacted with annoyance. "You dress as Chewbacca *one time* and all of a sudden you're labeled a furry! Do people not realize how hard it is to find costumes when you're my height?"

Maggie couldn't hold back her giggles. "Chewbacca? Really?"

Charles muttered, "I wore it to a *Star Wars* convention."

"No way! Charles Louden, famous stuffed shirt, is a *Star Wars* fan?"

"Stuffed shirt?" Charles smoothed his tie absentmindedly and looked hurt.

Maggie patted his hand.

"Anyway, I know how that rumor got started—I ran into some students from our department and, in a moment of weakness, let them take a picture. I should have known I couldn't trust them. They were dressed as stormtroopers." Charles sighed as Maggie giggled again. "But the difference between the rumors about me and the rumors about you is that rumors of my predilection for fur have been greatly exaggerated, whereas you..."

"What about me?"

"Well, you actually are dating Ms. Morgan. So that's not really a rumor. Though there is a rumor going around saying Rory's going to quit school to have your baby, and frankly, I'm not even sure how that would work exactly."

"I could explain if you want."

"No, no, I'll pass. But the rumors that really disturb me are the ones that claim you're a predator and have come on to other students."

"Charles, I have never—"

"I know that, I do. But this is what I was afraid would happen. Right now, it's just students talking, but it's only a matter of time before the board is asking for your head on a platter. I really don't want to see that happen. You're a good teacher."

"Thank you for saying so, Charles." They sat in silence a moment. Then, "All this because I'm in an unconventional relationship? Why can't people just mind their own business?"

"That's the question, isn't it? You know, I'm reminded of my old high school history teacher. He fell for one of his students. And there was a big age difference between them too, about twenty-five years or more, I think. Now, no one knew for sure if they really dated when she was still in school, but she wouldn't keep quiet about how much she loved him. You know what ol' Mr. Augustine did?" Maggie shook her head, fascinated. "A year after she graduated, he asked her to marry him. And they're still going strong. Two kids, both recently graduated college." Charles gave her a knowing look but said no more.

After a moment, Maggie asked, "Are you suggesting what I think you're suggesting?"

"That you make an honest woman of her? Do something that would give your relationship legitimacy? No, that's not in my job description. I'm just telling stories." Suddenly he stood up. "Well, I need to get going. The missus and I are going out tonight. Apparently. I'll see you later. Can't wait for opening night, looks great." Charles patted her on the shoulder as he made his way to the aisle, then proceeded to leave.

Maggie sat there in stunned silence, staring directly in front of her but seeing nothing. Married? Was he seriously telling her to do that? Why the change? Then it dawned on her. Charles wasn't being supportive at all; he was just trying to cover his ass. Hers too, maybe. But she would not be pushed into something as important as marriage just to appease a group of people to whom she owed nothing. Suddenly, Rory jumped off the stage in front of her, startling her out of her rumination. She looked up and gave Rory a small smile. "Do you know how loud those boots are when you do that?"

Rory grinned as she came closer. "Just making sure you're awake, Doc. There's some important theatering going on up there"—she pointed over her shoulder—"and I didn't want you to miss it."

"Doc again? Really?"

"Yeah. Thought you missed the nickname."

"Whatever gave you that idea?"

Rory shrugged. "Don't know." She sat in the seat Charles had vacated and looked into Maggie's eyes, really looked. Maggie held her gaze, unflinching. "You okay?"

Maggie nodded. "I am now. Thank you." She almost reached for Rory's hand but thought better of it and kept her hands in her lap.

Rory leaned in to whisper in Maggie's ear and said, "Calling you Doc or Dr. Parks in public is me saying *I love you* in a crowded room."

Maggie felt her face flush. Rory's grin confirmed just how noticeable the blush was. "Ms. Morgan, don't you have some important theatering to do?"

Rory laughed. "That's right, put me in my place."

"Well, I am your director, and that is my job."

Rory laughed again and stood up. She took a position in front of Maggie and bowed, as she had done onstage after many a performance. "As you wish, Dr. Parks, as you wish." With a wink, she turned and hopped back onstage.

Maggie just smiled and shook her head. Marriage to that hellion? Saints preserve us.

Chapter Fifteen

Opening night, Rory and Maggie arrived together. They had decided that, though they wouldn't flaunt their relationship, they wouldn't take extra pains to hide it anymore either.

On the way to the theater, Rory lamented that she had to wear a dress, much to Maggie's amusement. "I still don't see why we can't update it some so I could wear pants. That's the worst part. Before yesterday's dress rehearsal, I hadn't worn a dress since I was eight years old. And I'm proud of that fact, thank you very much."

"What was the occasion?"

"My Aunt Katherine's wedding. It was white with a blue ribbon or…sash…*thing* at my waist that everyone said went so nicely with my eyes. It just felt like I was wearing an itchy pillowcase or something. And the breeze up the skirt was not right at all. I kept fidgeting. I drove my mother crazy. I vowed from that day forward I would never wear a dress again. I was traumatized."

Maggie couldn't help laughing out loud. "You made this vow at eight, did you?"

"Oh yes. And kept it too, until now. Have you seen how low cut that thing is?"

Maggie eyed her lasciviously and replied, "Mm, yes, I have. I don't see a problem."

"You're objectifying me. I know my rights."

Laughing again, Maggie patted Rory on the knee reassuringly as they parked in the lot behind the theater.

Used to the anxieties and insecurities of actors, Maggie knew Rory's protests were more about opening-night jitters and less about feeling out of sorts in a dress, though she also understood that was a very real thing for Rory. "Honey, you're going to be beautiful. Don't worry." Maggie gave her a quick kiss.

"You mean I'm not going to look like a little Irish boy in a dress?"

"No, my love. You are going to show off just how beautiful you are." Maggie touched her hand to Rory's cheek, then kissed her there.

"Yeah, cause I'm going to be showing everything."

Maggie threw her head back in exasperation. "Come on, let's go." Rory was still muttering as they got out of the car. Maggie just took her hand and rolled her eyes.

❖

Maggie had her cast gathered around her backstage just before the curtain went up. "You guys are going to do so well. I'm proud of you all for how great you are. Now go out there and shine like the stars you are."

Arenda yelled, "Places!" and everyone scrambled to their marks or to the wings.

Maggie caught Rory's eye and winked. Rory smiled in return. Rory really was beautiful, Maggie thought. She knew she had better enjoy this look while it lasted, because she doubted she would ever see Rory in a dress again, unless a role demanded it. The ivory satin looked fabulous against Rory's alabaster skin. Maggie had asked wardrobe to moderate the plunge of Rory's neckline, a few quick stitches right before Rory got in costume. She had been granted a grateful smile from Rory for her thoughtfulness. Rory's hair was pulled back, for the first time since Maggie had known her, in a style Maggie had been amused to hear the hairdresser call a Princess Belle style; Rory had been aghast at yet another Disney princess reference. They had wisely done away with having her wear heels, as she would have towered over Davis and wouldn't have been able to walk in them anyway.

After the curtain went up Maggie peeked out into the audience and saw Rachel sitting with Rory's parents front row center, in the seats she had reserved for them. Davis's parents sat next to them. They all seemed to be enjoying the show. She focused on Rachel especially and saw the look on her face. Maggie could clearly read the love on her face as she watched Rory. She felt for the girl, she really did. It was one thing to know that Rachel loved Rory; it was another thing to see it so raw like that. She respected Rachel's strength and ability to keep up the shield of friendship, while the whole time feeling so much more.

Rory and Davis were a great team. The tension between them was so palpable they were almost uncomfortable to watch; it was like spying on them in their bedroom. Maggie could tell the audience was right with them. When the curtain came down on the final scene, the applause came up, loud and furious. The cast quickly assembled in a line with Rory and Davis in the center. When the curtain went up again they were all clasping hands and they bowed in unison. Then the supporting cast took a step back, leaving Rory and Davis center stage, and they bowed together. Arenda came out from stage right and presented Rory with a bouquet of long-stem red roses. Rory accepted them and, as was custom, took one rose out of the bouquet and presented it to Davis with a slight bow to him. When the curtain came down again, Rory gestured wildly to Maggie. She quickly pulled off her headset and tossed it to Arenda, then went forward and stood on Rory's left. As the curtain came up, the rest of the cast came forward again, and they all bowed together. When they all stood back up, Rory turned and gently placed the rest of the bouquet into Maggie's surprised arms.

Amidst the thunderous cheers and applause, Rory said, "You deserve these more than I do." Then she turned her back to the audience and bowed only to Maggie as a gentleman to a lady, with one arm behind her back. After she straightened, she noticed Davis and the rest of the cast had joined her to give Maggie the respect she deserved. Miranda was suddenly on Rory's right.

Just before they all bowed, Miranda said, "She's our director too, you know. We got your back." Then she winked.

Rory didn't have time to puzzle over it, but she thought she got it. If she had been the only one to bow to Maggie, it might look odd, even confirm all the rumors and get people talking all over again. That Miranda seemed to want to stop the gossip seemed weird, since Rory strongly suspected she had started the chatter in the first place. But she had no time for contemplation; she just bowed with the rest of the cast in praise of Maggie. She wasn't the only one who loved Maggie, she realized, but she swelled with pride because she alone had won this wonderful woman's heart.

❖

Once the curtain calls were over and done with, after foisting the flowers on poor Arenda, Maggie pulled Rory aside to a corner backstage and couldn't restrain herself from hugging her furiously. "Oh my God, that was wonderful."

Still clinging to Maggie, Rory asked, "Which part, the performance part, or the part where the whole cast mooned the audience?"

Maggie laughed. "All of it! I didn't expect the bow—that was very sweet. And you were especially wonderful."

"Shh, you do have other cast members, you know? Besides, you're biased."

"I'm allowed to be."

Some of the cast was still hanging around backstage. James, the actor who had played Big Daddy, walked by and said, "For God's sake, just kiss her already. We know." Everyone within earshot laughed.

Rory looked at Maggie, shrugged, then practically swept her off her feet in a tremendous kiss. Hoots and hollers came up from the cast and crew still milling about. Laughing, Maggie threw her arms around Rory's neck and held on for the ride.

"All right, enough of that. Nobody wants to see that." Rachel appeared from the wings with Rory's parents. Rory disengaged from Maggie to hug her parents in turn. "Good show, Dr. Parks...I mean, Maggie."

"Thank you, Rachel. I'm glad you came."

"Are you kidding? As the unofficial president of her unofficial fan club, I had to come."

Rory came up and put an arm around Rachel's shoulders. "When there's only one person in the club, it's not a club—then it's just called stalking."

"Not until you file a restraining order, it's not. Until then it's just fandom. Get used to it. When you're a famous actress, you'll have more fans. And they won't all be as sane as me."

"Lord help me."

Rory's father said, "Maggie, you did an excellent job getting a great performance out of the cast."

"Thank you, John. They were a great group to work with, especially your daughter."

"Maybe I'm biased, but I have to agree with you."

"Will you be directing another play next semester, Maggie?" Rory's mother asked.

"No, I'm going to be too busy. Teaching more classes, preparing for conferences, that sort of thing. Dr. Baskin will be doing a production, however."

"Did you say Dr. Baskin?" Rachel asked eagerly.

"Yes, I did. Why?"

"I just might have to audition."

"You don't even know what she's directing, it could be boring," Rory interjected.

"Rory, it doesn't matter, it's Dr. Sexy—I mean, Dr. Baskin."

Maggie and the Morgans just laughed.

"Don't you mean Dr. Straight Love?" Rory said.

"Details."

Rory looked at Maggie. "So what is the play, anyway?"

"*A Chorus Line.*"

"Really? Rachel, I think we should both audition. I would love to do that show."

"I'd love to stand onstage and sing about tits and ass."

"And I, my friend, would love to wear a top hat and tails."

"You do know that, as a girl, you wouldn't be wearing pants, right? You'd have to show off those long legs of yours, that no one has seen before tonight." Rachel reached down and mimed caressing Rory's leg in a playful manner, and Rory smacked her hand away.

"Excuse me?"

"Yes, excuse me?" Maggie gave her best stern look.

"Relax, I wasn't going above the knee."

"I am not a piece of meat, you know."

"Too bad, I'm getting hungry."

John stepped up. "Okay, lewd thoughts about my daughter aside"—he narrowed his eyes at Rachel, who suddenly looked chastened, then he winked at her and it made her smile—"she has a point. Let's go eat. Your mother's buying."

"Yes, but I'm using your credit card, dear."

"Of course, my love. Rory, how fast can you get out of this thing and back into your street clothes?"

"I thought you'd never ask. Quicker than you can say, *Rachel's a pervy stalker.*"

"I prefer superfan, thank you."

John put his arm around Rachel's shoulders and said placatingly, "Come on. If you're good I'll buy you an ice cream."

"With sprinkles?"

"Of course. Now let's let her change."

The Morgans and Rachel left together, leaving Rory and Maggie alone.

"Hey, Maggie Parks?"

"Yes, Rory Morgan."

"Damn fine show you put on here."

"Thank you, you too."

"Couldn't have done it without you."

"I know." Maggie grinned.

"I love you. Just that."

"That's all that matters." Her smile and the tears threatening to fall confirmed her words.

❖

Later that evening, after everyone else had finally left them alone, Rory and Maggie were lounging on Maggie's couch, too exhausted to move. Instead of snuggling, they each lay in their own corners, Rory's feet dangling off the couch, Maggie's propped across Rory's legs.

"Long day. But a good one," Rory said, as she absentmindedly rubbed Maggie's feet. Maggie had a contented smile on her face.

"Um, yes. You guys all did so great."

"Well, you made us great."

"Nonsense, I did little more than tell you where to stand."

"I will compliment you, dammit, and you're going to let me."

Maggie chuckled. "Is that really necessary?"

"Yes." Without warning, Rory grabbed the cuffs of Maggie's pants and pulled a very surprised Maggie out of her corner. She yelped in surprise, ending up lying on her back with Rory on top of her. Rory had the gleam in her eye that Maggie loved so much and she knew it meant mischief was afoot.

Maggie put her arms around Rory's neck and said, "I think I could get used to this." She pulled Rory to her for a kiss, glad that Rory's hair was now free so she could run her hands through it or give it a gentle tug.

"I thought you were tired."

"Hey, I didn't start this, remember? But I will damn well make sure you finish it." With that declaration, Maggie grabbed Rory's T-shirt with her fist and pulled her back down on top of her. "There, that's where you're supposed to be."

"You are becoming so feisty."

"I don't know what you're talking about. Now, shut up and get back to work."

"Damn. Okay then." Gently, she put her lips to Maggie's

earlobe and sucked on it for a moment, running her tongue around the outer edge because she knew it made Maggie squirm in the best way. Then she trailed kisses down to the hollow of Maggie's neck, where she began to nibble, and Maggie moaned. Encouraged, Rory changed from nibbling to gently sucking, occasionally grazing her teeth over a spot. The more effort she put into it, the louder Maggie moaned and pressed her head farther into her. After several moments, Rory pulled back some and looked at what she had done. She looked sheepishly down at Maggie. "Don't hate me."

Maggie laughed with pure joy. "Oh, my love, I haven't had a hickey in a very long time. I had forgotten how pleasant they can be. Thank you."

"Yeah, you may not be thanking me when you look in the mirror later."

"Tell me—is it big enough to make the busybodies in the department lose their shit?"

"Did you seriously just say *lose their shit*?"

"Yes, I did. Is it?"

"Um, yeah, I would say they probably won't be able to control themselves, yeah."

"Good, then it'll serve its purpose."

"And here I thought its only purpose was to give you pleasure. Have I been misinformed?"

"Oh no, it does that too. But it also sends an important message."

"Woman, there's the devil in you!"

"Not yet, she's not, but I keep hoping she'll stop talking soon and get inside me." Maggie laughed to see Rory's mouth hang open in shock.

"Such language."

"Uh-huh. No more talking." Maggie yanked Rory down to

her and kissed her so furiously that their teeth nearly collided. She let herself get lost in Rory's embrace and relaxed into the familiar feel of Rory's arms.

❖

The next morning, Maggie checked out Rory's handiwork in the bathroom mirror. The hickey was quite impressive, about the size of a half-dollar, and a deep crimson. It was placed just high enough that she'd have to wear a turtleneck to cover it, but she didn't actually own any. She chuckled at the thought of what her colleagues might think when they saw it. The further her relationship with Rory progressed, however, the less she cared what her coworkers thought.

She contemplated wearing her hair down, which she rarely did for work because, despite the potential satisfaction of seeing the faces of the naysayers, she was a professional adult who didn't need to prove she was getting laid. Besides, they all apparently knew that by now, anyway.

Rory came in from the bedroom and stood behind her. Maggie smiled at her in the mirror and Rory encircled Maggie's waist and kissed her on the shoulder. Maggie leaned into her and hugged her back.

"Good morning, beautiful," Rory said.

"You are really good at making me feel loved. Good job. A-plus."

"I aim to please, ma'am."

"Well, you do."

"Good." Rory moved Maggie's hair aside so she could get a better look at what she had done. "Wow, that got bigger than I thought it would."

"That's what she said." Maggie could barely contain her giggles.

Rory's mouth hung open. "I don't know who you are anymore."

Maggie turned around in Rory's embrace, put her arms around her neck, and gave her a slow, sensual kiss that made Rory moan, which made Maggie smile. "You're right to say I'm different. You're right, I am. I hope for the better."

"Well, it's not for the worse, that's for sure. Didn't say I didn't like the new you, just different."

"I see. You've helped me realize that I shouldn't take things so seriously all the time. And my colleagues have taught me that I don't give a damn what anyone thinks. I'm going to live my life the way I see fit. And I want that life to include you."

"A wise man once said to me, fuck 'em if they can't take a joke."

"Your friend was very wise and eloquent indeed."

"Yes, he was. Hey, speaking of being a part of each other's lives, I'm supposed to invite you home for Thanksgiving. You wanna come?"

Maggie sighed in a somewhat amused fashion. "You pick the best time to ask me about that. I'm standing in front of you naked and you want to talk about your family? Really?"

"I just remembered. I was thinking about other things last night and was distracted. I forgot."

"Oh, and you're not thinking about that now?" Maggie twirled one of Rory's curls around her finger and gave her a flirtatious look.

"Oh, I'm always thinking about that. And you standing in front of me splendidly naked is not helping my concentration one bit, but I am honor bound to deliver this message of invitation to you. So, what do you say?"

"Your parents' house for Thanksgiving? Would we be spending the night?"

"I usually stay the whole vacation, yeah."

"Are they going to let us sleep in the same bed?"

"Why wouldn't they?"

"Some parents get weirded out by it, no matter how accepting they might be. I just don't want anyone to feel awkward."

"Oh, I see. It never came up, actually."

"I'll tell you what—ask them about sleeping arrangements, and if we can share a room then I'll stay the whole weekend. If not, I'll go up for the day and come home, that way you don't miss out on time with your family. Sound reasonable?"

"Very much. Has anyone told you how awesome you are?"

"Not recently."

"Well, you are." Quick peck on the lips. "And sexy." Another quick peck. "And brilliant." Peck. "And beautiful." Peck. Before Rory could say another word, Maggie grabbed Rory's T-shirt in her fist and pulled her close.

"And fucking impatient." She pulled Rory to her and kissed her passionately. "I love you, Rory."

"Love you too."

Chapter Sixteen

With their relationship now out in the open, after a holiday season full of time spent with family and a whirlwind New Year's trip to Chicago, Maggie and Rory made things official. Maggie had surprised Rory with a key to her house on Christmas morning, and Rory moved out of the dorms and into Maggie's house before the spring semester began. When classes started again, Rory had a full load, three classes, which meant more work, but she loved it. She had always loved school, even as a child. In fact, she remembered the time before she could read and how angry she would get with herself for not being able to understand the words. When her mother would read to her, she would often look at the pictures and think her mother had changed the story, because the pictures didn't match what she had in her head. Once she learned to read the world opened up to her and books became her constant companions.

When she discovered acting, it suited her old need to match the words on the page to what she saw in her head. She loved expressing herself on the stage. It wasn't about the attention from the audience or a need for approval, which she knew some of her classmates thrived on. She didn't need the validation. What she did, she did for herself. She got enjoyment from a job well done and from playing the part. It was like grown-up dress-up, and she liked stepping into someone else's shoes, even if only for a night.

Instead of taking Stage Combat with Maggie, which she had been looking forward to, she was stuck taking the Movement class with Dr. Baskin instead. She was also taking a voice class, and she and Rachel were in an acting class together.

Living in Maggie's house was amazing. It was always quiet. There were no sudden bursts of yelling in the hallway, no communal showers, a kitchen that was all her own, and of course, the best part of all, there was Maggie. Knowing that she didn't have to pack up and go back to the dorm after a few days was such a wonderful feeling. On days she didn't have a class, she stayed in her pajamas all day, resting comfortably in the reading chair, feet up on the coffee table, propped on the décor books Maggie hadn't looked at in years, with a steaming mug of coffee beside her. And no matter her schedule, she cooked Maggie breakfast and dinner every day and packed her lunch in the blue and green thermal bag every day, with a different note of love or encouragement every time.

She really liked the domesticity of it all and had to keep reminding herself that this was now her life. Just a few months before, she had been a student with just another teacher crush, without much hope that anything would ever come from it. Now she got to spend every night with a woman she used to fantasize about but who she never thought she would ever get to know on a personal level, let alone win her heart and share her bed. To say she felt lucky was putting it mildly.

She was happy and content and, today, suddenly very sleepy. The night before, she and Maggie had stayed up late so she could introduce Maggie to one of her favorite shows, *Mystery Science Theater 3000*. Maggie had left the house that morning dragging, and Rory was thankful that she didn't have classes that day. When she started to fall asleep in the reading chair, she just let it happen, scooting down lower and letting the book fall over her chest.

❖

Maggie came home and found Rory sound asleep in the reading chair. Maggie smiled to see her there. Maggie quietly put her bag on her desk and walked over to the side of the chair and stood there for a moment, just taking it in. Today was a day Rory had decided not to get dressed, so she was wearing a plain T-shirt, flannel pajama pants, and plain white socks, an old flannel shirt on over the T-shirt to ward off the occasional chill that sometimes crept into the old house. Her book had slid down to her lap, her hands were crossed over it, and her chin was resting on her chest. She looked so vulnerable like that, Maggie thought, that she almost didn't want to disturb her. But it also made Maggie want to curl up next to her, and she couldn't do that in the chair, at least not comfortably.

Instead, she touched Rory's hand. "Honey, I'm home." Rory mumbled but otherwise didn't stir. Maggie tried again. "Rory, honey, time to wake up. If you want a nap, we can go to bed."

"Um...don't make me move. So comfortable."

"Really? This chair doesn't even recline. Come on. You want a nap, I'll go tuck you in." Maggie took the book off Rory's lap, closed it, and put it on the coffee table. Then she took Rory's hand and tried to pull her out of the chair.

Opening her eyes partway, Rory said, "Hi, baby," then she closed them again and sank back into the chair.

Maggie laughed and dropped her hand. "You're a lost cause, aren't you?"

"Mm-hmm." Rory curled up in the corner of the chair, her

feet extending farther onto the coffee table, knocking her book off in the process.

"Okay, sleep, I just hope you don't wake up all kinked up." Maggie placed a kiss on Rory's forehead and started to walk away, when Rory suddenly awoke more fully and sat up in the chair, a look of panic on her face.

"Oh, crap, I forgot about dinner." She started to get up and Maggie held up her hand.

"Hold on, you are not required to make dinner. If you're too tired, let me take care of it."

"No, I'm good. I can make dinner. I got this."

"Hey, I can call for takeout. Cooking for me, though a wonderful bonus, is not a condition of you living here. Relax, baby, I've got this."

Rory dropped back into the chair. "Sorry, I guess it's just become habit."

"And it's a good one, and I love it when you cook for me, but you are allowed to take a night off. What are you in the mood for?"

Suddenly Rory grinned at her and said, "Cheeseburgers."

Maggie returned her grin. "Then go put some pants on and we'll go get cheeseburgers."

"Our favorite place?"

"Of course."

"You're too good to me."

"I know, and don't you forget it."

❖

Rory and Maggie hadn't been to the old diner in months. The Miranda incident and all that followed had left a bad taste in their mouths and had kept them from going back to a place that they had both come to love, a place Rory thought of as where they'd had their first date. Maggie preferred to say their first date was the night they danced in their living room, but Rory thought of that as their first kiss. Either way, the little diner held mixed memories for them, but the truth was they did serve the best burgers in town, with the best atmosphere. Every time they were there Maggie felt that she should have been in a poodle skirt. At least now, in the leather biker jacket Maggie had gotten her for Christmas, Rory looked the part and fit in nicely with the fifties décor.

"Damn, you look good in that jacket."

Rory blushed and averted her eyes, then grinned, but her embarrassment was still visible. "Thank you. I thought it appropriate."

"Oh, and it is. A very wise choice, indeed. You look like a greaser punk."

"Hey, I know I haven't showered today, but I wouldn't call my hair greasy."

Maggie laughed. "You know what I mean. I just meant you look like you belong here, like you're a part of this time and place." Maggie shook her head. "I don't think I'm saying it very well."

"No, I get it. And I take that as a compliment, as I'm sure you know. I know the fifties weren't really as awesome as we've glamorized them to be over the years, but I do relate to this era. The old-style butch, you know? When it was still okay to have manners and treat a woman like a lady. To fight for your lady's honor and stand proud against any asshole, even if he was a cop. To work hard and use your hands to make your living. To hang out in a neighborhood bar, have a beer, shoot a game of pool, and bitch about work or dance with your lady to some slow song. And wear awesome jackets." Rory grinned as she took a bite of her burger.

"My love, your fantasy is wonderful, but quite frankly,

I'm glad that time is past. Baby, you would have been beaten up and I would have been the one to put you back together. I don't know if I would have been able to deal with that."

"Trust me—I don't take any of my current privilege for granted. I just meant that I think we're losing an important part of our culture. The old guard of butches is disappearing and my peers are doing butch in different ways, when there was nothing wrong with the old ways."

Maggie laughed, but not unkindly. "You really do have an old soul, my love, and I love that about you." Maggie took a sip of her milk shake, a must every time they were at the diner. Then she became thoughtful. "You do know I'm not exactly a lady, and that you don't have to fight for my honor, right?"

Rory laughed out loud. "Yes, I do know that. I have a feeling you could kick my ass, if you so chose, and anyone else's too, for that matter. I knew from day one you were a badass—you don't have to convince me. Just one of the things I was attracted to."

"Really, you knew that from day one? How could you tell?"

"I don't know, you just have a certain way you carry yourself that says you mean business. The way you move, it's kind of dangerous."

"Dangerous? What do you mean by that?"

Rory shrugged. "Just that you carry yourself in a way that says you can handle yourself in any situation. Kind of a strut, but not a cocky one, more like a confident one because you know what your abilities are and you want others to know them too. That just because you're small, people shouldn't dismiss you. It's really sexy, actually."

"Oh, I see."

"You didn't know this about yourself, did you?"

"Well, no one has ever described me as dangerous before."

"Then they weren't paying close enough attention. And I'm disappointed I won't get to learn all those cool stage combat techniques from you. Or see you wield a sword. I would love to see my little Mighty Maggie wield a sword." Rory snickered.

"I was going to offer to teach you anyway, but not if you're going to be a brat about it. You can just find someone else to show you all those cool things." Rory stuck her tongue out at her and it made Maggie laugh.

A few minutes later, Rory excused herself to use the restroom, and a moment after she left the table, Maggie looked up to see Miranda approaching her table. She plastered on a smile. "Hello, Miranda."

Miranda looked nervous. "I just wanted to apologize. I should have never sent that picture. It was such a bitchy thing to do, and I'm sorry. I hope it didn't get you in trouble with the dean or anyone."

Surprised at the sudden confession, Maggie quickly found her voice. "No, not really. I just have one question though— why? Why did you do it?"

"I wanted to go out with her and…well, it just got messed up. I just want you to know that I hope things work out for you two. I mean that."

Maggie could tell that Miranda was struggling to find the right words, so she held up her hand. "I appreciate you saying that. Thank you. Just think next time about the consequences before you act."

"Okay."

Maggie caught the scowl on Rory's face as she headed back toward their table, and she knew from Miranda's expression that she'd seen it too.

"I should go." Miranda quickly left and was back at her table by the time Rory reached theirs and sat down, but not before giving Miranda a glaring look.

"What did she want?"

"It's not what you think. She wanted to apologize."

Rory looked surprised. "Seriously?"

"Yes. I think she was hurt when you wouldn't go out with her and she acted on impulse. Things just got out of hand."

"Still, that doesn't give her the right to do something so heinous. It's one thing to talk shit about me, but she could have jeopardized your job. Forgive her if you want, but I don't think I can."

"I think she's trying to make amends. I think she realizes that it was a stupid thing to do and wishes she had made different choices. It took a lot of courage for her to come over here."

"Yeah, but then she scurried away when I came back. She's afraid of me."

"Well, do you blame her? You did look menacing when you came back to the table, my love."

"Menacing, really?" Rory looked as if she liked the sound of that.

Maggie laughed. "Yes, you did. Imagine what she saw: you coming at her, nearly six feet tall in your boots, that jacket, a scowl on your face. I'd have run away too, even if I hadn't done anything wrong."

"I'm not sure if I should take that as a compliment, or if I should apologize. I mean, the last thing I want to do is make you afraid of me."

"Did I say I was afraid of you? I just meant that you can look downright intimidating when you want to. It's kind of sexy, actually."

"Oh. Well, that's okay then. I still don't know if I can forgive her, though."

"My love, don't waste time on things like that. It happened, we've moved on from it, and nothing bad happened. In fact, something good came from it."

"Really, like what?"

"Like, it forced me to realize how I feel about you and to stop running from it."

"So, in essence, her plan backfired, and in a way, we have her to thank for us getting together in the first place?"

"In a manner of speaking."

"Well, that's one way of looking at it. I'll try to see it from your point of view, Maggie Parks."

When they were finished with their meal and were on their way out, Rory caught Miranda's eye and inclined her head in a conciliatory manner. She thought of the night of the play, how Miranda had been one of the first at her side to bow to Maggie during the final curtain call. And she realized that what Maggie had said was true. While Rory would never forget what Miranda had done, she appreciated she was trying to make amends. Rory figured the least she could do was meet her halfway. Miranda looked nervous at first, but finally gave her a small smile. In just those few moments, Rory thought they had closed an important chapter.

Chapter Seventeen

Things settled into a routine for Maggie and Rory. Despite their busy schedules, they made sure to make time for each other every day. Whenever possible, they went out on the weekends, mostly hanging out with Bill and Dix, but sometimes just the two of them, date nights. They had Rachel over for dinner once every couple of weeks. She still wasn't saying much about what she was doing in her off time, though Rory suspected she was seeing someone and just didn't want to talk about it. Life was finding its groove and Rory and Maggie were fitting into it just fine.

Halfway through the semester, Maggie received an email—apparently from a colleague, although it was unsigned and sent from an anonymous account. Maggie wasn't sure whether to be amused or horrified as she read:

Margaret,
It has come to my attention and, quite frankly, to the attention of everyone else in the department, that you are conducting yourself in a most egregious, immoral way by having an improper relationship with a student, and you have further compounded your error by moving that impressionable young girl into your home. There are many of us who are

concerned, not only for the well-being of the girl in question, but for other students who may have fallen prey to you before, as well as those who might fall victim to you in the future, should you become tired of your current paramour.

Don't get me wrong, we are not judging your homosexual lifestyle, which we have all known about for years. Rather, we are merely concerned for those students who have been entrusted into your care. We ask that you cease and desist with this relationship, or we will be forced to take our concerns to the dean and the board. Again, please understand that we are only thinking of the children and Ms. Morgan in particular.

We are sure you are aware of the impropriety of such a relationship and the problems it poses regarding consent and power dynamics. We, your concerned colleagues, are just trying to maintain the integrity of this department. And you should be concerned with maintaining the respect you have currently achieved in your position as full professor in this institution.

With all due respect and concern,
A Theater Department Faculty Member

Many things came to Maggie's mind that she knew she shouldn't say, but she was pissed. How dare they, under the guise of being concerned for the students, try to tell her what to do? And thinking they had Rory's best interest in mind? The fucking nerve! They had no right! Fucking hypocrites, the lot of them. And to imply that she was a predator was going beyond any realm of decency. That's the part that really got to her. She had never done, nor would she ever do anything improper with a student. Everything had always been consensual with Rory and there had never been any other students in the past that had remotely interested her romantically or sexually. Until Rory, she too had looked on even her grad students as barely adults, not potential partners.

But the truth was, almost everyone in the department had been part of some mini-scandal over the years, from extramarital affairs, to drugs and alcohol, to their own children behaving badly. Maggie had ignored all the gossip, had never taken part in the rumor mill. She didn't care; she knew everyone had their own struggles and challenges, and she'd always thought those things should not be up for public scrutiny. All this concern for the students was just a thinly veiled homophobia, as well as a spitefulness that Maggie didn't understand. Apparently, the entire department was made up of mean girls.

But then another ding signaled a new email in her inbox. She opened it with dread. It was from Dr. Baskin, someone she spoke to, when their paths crossed at meetings or in the hallway, but had never been close to. Some of her colleagues avoided Dr. Baskin because she'd had an affair with a married colleague, Mark, who eventually left his wife for her, but Margaret had nothing personal against her. They just didn't have much in common. Sara Baskin was a very boisterous woman, with a booming laugh that made everyone turn in her direction to see what was so funny. When she entered a room, she consumed the space, while Maggie was more the type to just casually walk in. Maggie had never admitted it to anyone, but she found Dr. Baskin just as sexy and intimidating as the students did.

Margaret,

My guess is you've received an email from the tight-ass contingent, who feel it's their sworn duty to uphold the integrity of this fine institution by telling the rest of us what to do. I'm sure it was prim and proper and full of nicely worded snark. I just wanted to tell you that not all of us feel that way. You have friends here.

When Mark and I started dating, I received the same type of email. They felt our relationship was just too much for the tender little souls in our care. Meanwhile, those tender little souls probably know more about sex and relationships than we could ever hope to know and not only are they not traumatized by the soap opera of our lives, they couldn't give a rat's ass.

So don't lose hope. They have no power here, except to make you miserable. Don't let them. I've seen the change in you since she came into your life. You smile more, for one. And she's in my class this semester, of which I'm sure you're aware. I've always found her a bright, engaged student, but she too seems different. Happy. I know this relationship is one of mutual consent and, it appears, great love. Just as Mark's and mine is. That's what they really can't stand—to see people happy. It has been said that happiness is the best revenge.

I'm with you,
S.

This email almost made Maggie cry grateful tears. She sent a quick thank you, not able to say much more than that. She wanted Sara to know she appreciated her kind words. Then, fortified with the good feelings, she responded to the first email with a clear head:

Dear Anonymous Colleague:
I appreciate your kind words about my reputation

and I share your concerns about the students in our care. I agree with you that no harm should come to them and I deplore anyone who would use their position of power over students to force them to do things they normally would not want to do, as I've heard Dr. Stuart has done on several occasions.

And I'm sure when Ms. Morgan learns of your concern on her behalf, she will be most grateful that you are looking out for her best interests. But you have my assurance that nothing untoward is happening, nor have I used my position of power to force Ms. Morgan to make decisions she would not have made otherwise.

I have been in contact with the dean and he is aware of my present circumstances and we have had many a discussion on the matter. Also, the Christmas holiday spent with Ms. Morgan's parents was most enjoyable.

Again, I appreciate all of your concerns, but really, don't bother. I've got it covered. So please, cease and desist with further advice on the matter. If I should come upon a thorny situation and need to seek your assistance, I know where to find you.

Still morally and ethically yours,

Dr. Margaret Parks

Smiling to herself, Maggie hit send. Then she texted Rory: *You should know there are professors in our department who are concerned for you. One just emailed.*

A moment later, Rory replied: *How wonderful! I'm glad they care so much. But really, I'm fine.*

I have informed them of this. I think they may voice their concerns again.

*Don't worry. We'll get through this. After a while, some
other scandal will break and they'll forget all about you. Soon
enough we'll be yesterday's news.*

I can't wait for that day.

It'll happen. I love you.

I love you too. Until that day came, Maggie dreaded what
the nosy lot could do and how much havoc they could cause.

❖

After a few days of not hearing anything from the campus
moral authority, as Maggie had taken to thinking of them, she
thought that maybe they had gotten bored with her alleged
impropriety and moved on. Once, when she went into the
department office to check her campus mail, two colleagues
were there discussing a new hire. Apparently, he was very
young and inexperienced and they didn't have much hope for
him. She had no idea if these colleagues had been part of the
judgmental horde, but from the sneer in their voices, she had a
feeling they might have been.

She had to pass them on her way out, and she felt
compelled to say, "You know, with all the gossip that goes on
in this place, it's a wonder any teaching gets done at all."

The women looked at her and gave her a polite smile that
didn't reach their eyes. "I know, one would think. I just think
of the gossip as a welcome distraction from everything."

"There are better distractions."

One of the women could barely suppress her giggles. "So
we've heard."

Incensed, it was all Maggie could do to hold her tongue
and not let fly something she would deeply regret. Instead, she
stood in front of them and gave them a sweet smile. "If you'll

excuse me, I have office hours starting soon." She had almost escaped, when she heard her name being called.

"Ah, Margaret, I thought I heard your voice. Been wanting to talk to you."

Maggie turned around to face Charles, who was standing anxiously in his doorway. It took everything she had not to roll her eyes at him and say out loud, "Not this again." But, instead, she was a grown-up about it and gave him the same sweet smile she had given her colleagues. "Well, this is fortunate, then. What's up, Charles?"

"Come on in. We'll discuss it in here." Charles looked at the other two professors and nodded. "Ladies." Then he closed his door behind Maggie, who took a seat in front of his desk. As he was going back around his desk, he asked, "So, how've you been?"

"Charles, I feel that I can speak openly with you."

"Yes, I have always hoped so."

"Good. Now cut the crap, what's going on now?"

Charles gave her a small smile as he leaned back in his chair, his hands folded over his stomach, the picture of calmness. "You were never this cavalier when you were speaking to me. I imagine it's Ms. Morgan's influence."

"You can imagine it."

"Right. Well, there's no need to stand on formality. You know why you're here."

"Honestly, Charles, I really don't. I have upheld all of my job duties, even attended all those boring meetings that just waste my time, and yet there are some people who don't seem to care about that and, instead, seem to think they have a say in my love life. Well, since nothing I've done falls in the criminal realm, I would say that what I do in my off time is my business."

"Are you finished?"

"For now."

Charles leaned forward in his chair. "Look, I hear you, I'm on your side. But there's a noisy contingent that's screaming about moral turpitude and asking for your tenure to be revoked."

"What? Because of Rory? Ridiculous."

"You know how hard it is to get tenure revoked. They really don't have much to stand on. Plus, it's not as if you're the first member of the faculty to have a relationship with a grad student."

"Then why is this even an issue? Why are you even giving them the time of day? Can't you shut them down?"

"I can voice my opinion on the matter, but they can always go over my head, you know that. Even if they do, I seriously doubt that you would be fired. Any board wants to make damn sure they've got a solid case before they even consider going down that path."

"That's the polite way of saying they don't want to get sued."

"Well, that's always a concern."

"Charles, I already have grounds for a formal complaint against the colleagues who've been trying to make my situation impossible. But I'm just trying to live my life here, so I've been trying to let it go. Why can't they? Don't they have better things to do? I know I do."

"You're absolutely right. When I met with them, I asked them to stop, that they had no case to make. That they needed to leave you alone. I just don't think anything I said had any effect. I wanted to talk to you as a heads-up to let you know what's coming."

"I make no apologies for any decisions I've made up to this point or may be forced to make in the future."

"What do you mean by that?"

"I told you once before, I will not work someplace that puts so much scrutiny on my personal life. Maybe the optics were bad at the beginning, but when Rory was still my student, we watched the boundaries of our relationship. I know how wrong it is to sleep with a student, Charles, I'm not blind to that fact. And the suggestion that I'm a predator? I've never come on to a student in my life, and this time was no exception."

Amused, Charles asked, "Are you saying Ms. Morgan pursued you?"

Realizing what she had admitted, Maggie's face grew warm. "Actually, yes."

"You could have said no."

"I did."

"What changed your mind?"

"Initially? You."

"Me?"

"Yes, you sent me that email basically telling me to stop seeing her, which, in retrospect, was probably your way of trying to keep something like this from happening." Charles nodded to concede she had a point. "Honestly, that pissed me off. If I was going to get accused of it, I might as well do what I had wanted to do all along. So in a way, Charles, you were responsible for us getting together in the first place."

"Well, I'm flattered. I hope I get an invite to the wedding."

Maggie gave a surprised laugh. "I think it's a little too early to be thinking about that. But after our talk, I did think about it. It's just too soon. And quite frankly I don't want that decision to be made simply as a means to get people to stop talking about me. It's much more important than that."

"So would you seriously leave?"

"Charles, this is straight-up harassment. No one deserves this. I can't work like this."

"You would leave without a fight?"

"I'm tired of it, Charles. There's a part of me that knows I haven't done anything wrong and just wants to be left alone, but there's another part that knows the reality of the situation. Plus, I don't want to spend my time fighting just to live openly. I want to do my job, love openly, and mind my own business. Why can't they do the same?"

"I wish I knew what to tell you. Just don't let them defeat you."

"Whatever decision I make won't be about them defeating me. It'll be me living my life for me and not them. I'm tired of letting other people think they have a say in my life." She stood to leave. "Was that all?"

"I suppose so. Good luck, Margaret."

"Call me Maggie." She grinned as she left his office, though she didn't quite feel it.

❖

In retrospect, Maggie could understand where Charles had been coming from all this time. She finally understood the position he was in and respected where he was coming from; she just hoped he respected her position as well.

She got through the rest of her day, but barely. When she got home, Rory was in the kitchen, making dinner. The smells in the house were wonderful, and Maggie followed her nose to the kitchen to find Rory at the counter, chopping onions and garlic. She stood in the doorway and watched her for a moment, arms crossed over her chest. How could anyone think they had a right to say anything against this? It was love, pure and simple, no apologies, no regrets.

Without pausing in her chopping, Rory said, "I know you're back there, stalker."

Surprised, Maggie laughed. "How'd you know?"

Rory put the knife down, wiped her hands on a kitchen towel, and came over to Maggie in the doorway. "I heard the front door, then I smelled your perfume." Rory gave Maggie a critical once-over and touched her face. "You okay?"

Maggie sighed. "It's been a day. I'm just glad to be home."

Rory put her arms around Maggie and drew her to her. Maggie returned the hug, holding Rory as close as she could, wishing she could stay in the embrace the rest of the night. Rory whispered, "Want to tell me about it, my love?"

"Not much to tell. Just more of the same. Charles did call me into his office to warn me that they want to go over his head to the board. They want to revoke my tenure."

Rory pushed away to arm's length. "What in the hell? They can't just ask for your fucking tenure because they don't like who you're sleeping with, those tight-assed, jealous bastards. They're just pissed they can't get students to sleep with them. They can't do that. We won't let them."

"There may not be much we can do. They're free to go to the board if they wish."

"And claim...what? That you slept with a grad student who was perfectly willing and who dropped your class, of her own free will, the very next day?"

"None of that matters. There's a morals clause in my contract. This means I have to conduct myself in a moral way, and that can be interpreted in various ways. Quite frankly, whether you consented or not may not even matter. The facts will not matter, stacked up against the responsibility I hold as the one in a position of authority." Maggie sighed again, weary of it all.

"Well that's bullshit. I not only consented, I started it. If I hadn't, we probably wouldn't have happened at all."

Despite everything, Maggie was laughing. "You and I know that, love, but they have enough to make a case."

"No, they don't. I'm an adult who fell in love with her teacher and chased her. And got her." Rory placed a kiss on Maggie's lips. "Maggie, I firmly believe that this love was meant to be. Who cares how we met? Who cares about the age difference? Sometimes things just happen that way. This is our time. So, it doesn't fit into their plan? Who the fuck are they? They don't get a say in this. Let them go to the board—we'll fight."

"I don't know if I want to."

"Are you kidding? Are you just going to let them walk all over you? They're bullies, nothing but overgrown bullies who should know better. We can't let them win."

"Even if they don't win, we could still lose."

"How do you figure?"

"They can seriously damage me just by accusing me of things that aren't true. There are always going to be people who want to believe the worst of others. We've already seen that to be true." Maggie lightly pushed Rory away. "Excuse me, baby, I need a drink."

"Let me get it." Rory went to the cabinet for a wineglass and then grabbed the bottle of Maggie's favorite from the fridge, which Rory always made sure to keep chilled. It was one of the little courtesies that Maggie noticed and was grateful for. Rory handed the glass to Maggie with a smile. "Here you go, my love."

Maggie returned her smile. "Thank you." She took a welcome sip. "That was definitely needed. Might want to switch out my coffee for wine from now on."

"No, my love, I will not have you becoming an alcoholic on my watch."

"Watch me." Maggie grinned as she took another sip.

Once fortified, she spoke again of the problem at hand. "I don't want to give up. I just don't think this is something I should have to fight for in the first place."

"So what's the alternative? We all know bullies do not go away if you ignore them. They just double their efforts until they break you. I don't want you broken."

Maggie looked at Rory tenderly, moved by the look of determination mixed with love on her face. She took Rory's hand as Rory leaned against the counter. "Honey, they're not going to break me. I'm not going to let them. As you say, ignoring bullies doesn't make them go away, but showing them you're not afraid of them and that they have no power over you does."

"And how are you going to do that?"

"I don't know yet. But there's got to be some middle ground between giving up and beating the snot out of them."

Rory raised her hand, the one Maggie wasn't holding, as if she were in class, "Ooh, I vote for beating the snot out of them. Can I, can I, can I?"

Laughing, Maggie set her drink on the counter and put her arms around Rory's neck. "Not yet. I have something else I want you to do instead."

Rory put her arms around her and said, "My love, it would be my pleasure to take you to the bedroom right now and slowly cover your body with the tenderest of kisses and show you just how much I love you. But there's something else I have to do first." She said it all softly and when she was done she planted a long, leisurely kiss on Maggie's lips.

When they parted, Maggie asked, "What could you possibly have to do that would be more important?"

Rory chuckled as she trailed kisses along Maggie's neck. Between kisses, she said, "Turn off the stove."

Maggie laughed and took Rory's head in her hands, which

stopped her progress. "Okay, you have a point there, but that's the only thing you get to do. Come on. I don't know if I need you to make love to me, or to just lie there and love me." She took Rory's hand to lead her out of the kitchen.

"I know, my love. I know exactly what you need."

Maggie stopped and looked at her. "You do, don't you?"

"Always do. Come on." Rory turned off the burners on the stove on their way out of the kitchen. Now it was Rory's turn to lead Maggie out of the room. She took her to their room, laid her gently back on the bed, slowly removed Maggie's clothes, then her own, then stretched out next to her so they were skin to skin. She trailed her lips and fingers over every part of Maggie's body, letting no place go untouched. It was a long and languorous process, and by the time Rory was done and had come up to cradle Maggie in her arms, Maggie had never felt more loved.

Chapter Eighteen

The next day during Maggie's office hours, the phone on her desk rang. Her office number was only used by students and departmental colleagues, no one who knew her personally ever used that line, so she was surprised when she answered and heard a familiar voice, a voice she hadn't heard in years.

"Hello, Margaret."

"Max, how are you?"

"I always hated that nickname, you know that."

"Sorry, I was surprised, it just slipped out. How are you?"

"I'm fine. I didn't call to talk about me, however. I called to talk about you."

"Oh?"

"Yes. Are there really no single lesbians left in that town? Did you have to go after a student?"

Stunned, Maggie wasn't sure how to reply at first. "Excuse me?"

"Don't act like you don't know what I'm talking about. I still have friends on campus, you know. They've kept me informed about what's been going on lately. I mean, really? You should know better, you of all people. Is she even old enough to drink? I mean, geez, Margaret."

"Apparently, your spies have not given you all the information. Let me fill in the blanks for you." Maggie stood up and paced back and forth in her tiny office as much as the corded phone allowed, every word clipped. "She is, in point of fact, twenty-five, not my student, and I did not *go after* her. And I don't see how any of this is your business. Why did you even call, anyway? Just to give me your incredibly unwanted opinion of something that doesn't concern you in the slightest? Or to tell me I shouldn't be doing what I have every right to do? Again, your opinion is not needed."

"Calm down, I—"

"Calm down? Let me tell you something, in the history of pissed-off people, not once has anyone ever calmed down because someone told them to. And I have every right to be upset. And you have no right to call me, just so you can tell me you're disappointed in me. I don't give a rat's ass, Max. Again, my relationship is none of your business."

"I didn't call you to tell you how I feel about it, I called to warn you."

"Warn me?"

"They want you fired. They're going to the board about it."

"I know. Not much I can do about it. I can't stop them."

"You could stop seeing her."

"Nope, not going to happen. Not an option. Now, if you don't mind, I have to get back to work."

"Margaret, I'm just concerned for you, is all. I don't want you to lose your job over some fling. I know how much it means to you." Maggie thought she heard a note of sadness in Maxine's voice.

"This isn't some fling, Max. I love her. And no one has a say in this relationship but us. Whatever happens with the board, I will handle it. Sometimes, you have to realize what's most important, and it's not the job."

There was silence between them for a moment. "Why couldn't you have come to that conclusion years ago?"

"Because back then there wasn't anything more important than my job." The truth of that statement hit her hard. For the first time, Maggie fully realized that she had never loved Maxine the way she loved Rory. For Rory, she would give up the job she had sacrificed so much for. Not because she didn't love her job, she did. She loved making a difference in students' lives. She loved passing on knowledge to eager young minds. But she could do that anywhere. Tenure was a lovely security blanket, but it meant nothing without someone to share it with. Without Rory to go home to, it was just a tiny, drafty house. With Rory, it was a home. It had never been that with Maxine.

"I see. Fine, make your own mistakes. I won't warn you again. You're on your own."

"No, I'm not. Just because I don't have you in my life does not mean I'm on my own."

"You seriously think that child is going to know how to handle things when it all goes to hell? She hasn't experienced the world yet—she doesn't know anything about life. What comfort could she possibly be to you?"

"That child, as you call her, knows more than you ever did about what it means to love someone, and that's all she needs to know. I'm done listening to you. Good-bye, Max." Without waiting for a reply, she slammed the phone down and hoped it hurt on Maxine's end. She had always felt it was much more satisfying to slam a phone down at the end of a bad call than to just hit the end call button.

After all these years, Maxine had picked this to call about. Maggie shook her head. Max hadn't called when Maggie's father died and she could have used a friend. No, she called now to tell Maggie she disapproved of her choices, as if she had a say in anything. With friends like these, who needed enemies? Sighing, she texted Rory: *I just want you to know I appreciate everything about you, but most especially, how much you love. I am so lucky to be loved. I love you so much.*

There isn't an emoji big enough to tell you how big my heart just got. I don't know what you're currently going through today, but whatever it is, I got your back and I love you.

I know, my love. I never doubt that. I'll see you tonight.

It took her several minutes to put the call out of her head and to focus on the grading she had been doing before the phone call. "Okay, back to work. Evil spirits out!" she said to the empty room, as she refocused on the stack of essays on her desk.

❖

Maggie decided, after much thought, that she wasn't going to make some grand gesture to try to stop her colleagues from doing what they wanted to do. She didn't think anything would come from all their bluster, so, she figured, let them go marching into HR or even the president's office if they felt compelled to do so. She would just go about her business and not pay them any mind.

Meanwhile, she started to apply for jobs at other schools. What she had said to Charles was true; she couldn't work under the constant scrutiny of a noisy few who thought they had a right to voice their objections about her life choices. She wanted to find a place that would allow her to be herself and not care what she did when she was not at work. She had imagined theater departments would be more open and accepting than other departments. But in fact, not everyone was Sara Baskin or Bill. Maggie was done with it.

A part of her wanted to stand up to her bullies and make them see the error of their ways, to stop them from doing it to others. But she just didn't have the energy to change anyone's mindset. She appreciated Rory's bravado, but it just wasn't worth it. She felt powerless to change them. She wasn't ignoring them and hoping they went away, but she was trying to show them that they didn't scare her. That by going about her business and not hiding or stopping, she was telling them, "Do your worst, I can take it."

❖

A few weeks later, Maggie's attitude was vindicated. Charles informed her the board had shut her attackers down and, furthermore, warned them that their harassment of Maggie exposed them and the university to any number of workplace discrimination complaints. Grudgingly, Maggie imagined, the group went back into the hole they had crawled out of and resumed their normal lives, probably waiting for their next victim—though, according to Charles, the president himself gave them a verbal beat down about their assumed moral authority. That was one meeting Maggie regretted not being at.

Despite the satisfaction of knowing she had the support of not only some of her colleagues, but, as she finally understood, her dean, Maggie no longer wanted to work in a department that would harbor such petty people. When a small, private liberal arts college in Minnesota responded to her job application with an interview request, Maggie quickly accepted.

Rory wanted to accompany her on the five-hour road trip, but Maggie needed to make this trip on her own. Rory didn't try to argue, but she did pout about it a bit.

The night before heading to Minnesota, Maggie held

Rory in bed after she had spent some time showing her just how much she loved her. Rory's head lay against Maggie's chest, her arm was around her waist, and Maggie was holding her tight.

Rory sighed. "I'm going to miss you."

Maggie chuckled. "I'm only going to be gone one night."

"And part of Saturday."

"Yes, my love, but you only have to sleep without me once. You can handle that."

"Hardly. Remember how I was over finals last semester? I was a wreck. I'm sure I won't sleep at all."

"You are such a drama queen."

"Yeah, well, I'm not just me anymore, I'm you too. When you're not next to me, half of me is missing. That's why I can't sleep."

"Oh, honey…" Maggie squeezed Rory tighter and Rory snuggled closer. "I feel the same, but sometimes couples have to spend time apart."

Rory looked up at her. "But we don't have to. I could go with you. I'm not trying to sound all pathetic or make you feel bad, I promise. Just saying."

"I know. And me wanting to take this trip alone has nothing to do with you. Just something I want to do for myself. I need time alone in my own head to make sure I'm doing the right thing. Don't worry, whatever ends up coming from this, if anything, you will always be there. Okay?"

"I know. I don't doubt that anymore."

"I'll call you, text you, email you. I won't be far away."

"And Skype, so we can do dirty, dirty things."

Maggie laughed out loud. "We'll see about that one."

"Seeing…that's the whole point." Rory straddled Maggie, leaned over her, and gave her a powerful kiss. When she came away, they were both breathing heavily. There was an evil glint in her eye when she said, "Allow me to demonstrate." She then proceeded to show Maggie what they could do, long distance or not.

❖

The next morning, Maggie hit the road early, so that she could have plenty of time to check in to her hotel and freshen up before her interview. Rory made her a breakfast to go and filled her go-cup with coffee, then walked her to the car, in bare feet with no jacket, wearing only a T-shirt and flannel pajama pants.

"Aurora Morgan, you are going to catch your death out here." As she hugged her, Maggie rubbed Rory's arms and back to warm them up.

Rory laughed. "I'm fine. You look like you're freezing, though."

"I am. That's how I know you must be frozen solid. Hurry up and kiss me good-bye so you can get back in the house."

"I'm fine. But I will kiss you." Rory cupped Maggie's cheek and kissed her softly, then smiled. "I love you, Dr. Parks. Drive safe and come home to me as soon as you can."

"Mm, you have my word. I love you too. I'll call as soon as I arrive and then after the interview."

"And at bedtime, and when you leave in the morning."

Maggie chuckled. "You're going to get tired of talking to me that much."

"No, I won't. I never do." Rory pulled her iPod out of her pocket. "I made you a playlist for the drive."

"Thank you, my love. Too bad you won't be singing along."

"You want to be sung to, just call me and I'll sing for you."

"I think that would distract me too much. Okay, I should go. Love you. Now, get back in the house and warm up. Maybe go back to bed—it's early and you don't have anywhere to be today."

"You're not the boss of me. I do what I want." She grinned and Maggie pretended sternness.

"Young woman, don't make me turn you over my knee."

"I'd like to see you try." Still grinning, Rory backed away as Maggie jokingly made to come after her. From a safe distance, Rory said, "I love you too, now get out of here."

Going back to her car, Maggie warned, "Watch yourself, Morgan, I know where you live." With one final wave to Rory, who waved back from the porch, Maggie started the car and backed out of the driveway. Rory stayed on the porch until she couldn't see the car anymore, and only then did she go back inside to warm up. Freezing, she ran back to their bedroom, climbed back under the covers, and snuggled into the spot Maggie normally occupied. Hugging Maggie's pillow to her, she surprised herself by falling back asleep.

❖

The drive was boring but Maggie amused herself by listening to the playlist Rory had made for her. Maggie had to laugh when, at seven in the morning, her eardrums were blasted with AC/DC singing "Highway to Hell." She couldn't help but tap along on the steering wheel and shake her head at Rory's song choice. Maggie didn't normally listen to heavy metal, but she had to admit, she liked it. Rory's sense of humor showed itself again and again in the song choices, and Maggie laughed again when Rod Stewart sang to his Maggie May.

Much of the song was so appropriate to their situation, she couldn't help but enjoy it. She started to sing along.

"Maggie May, am I? Oh, my love, you are going to pay for that one."

The rest of the trip was filled with more fast beats which made the drive lively and fun. After checking in to her hotel, which wasn't that far from campus, she freshened up and changed into her interview clothes. Before she left, she texted Rory: *Your Maggie May has made it safe and sound.*

Maggie headed over to the campus and soon found herself waiting for her interview with Dean James. She tried not to appear nervous, but it had been a while since she had a job interview. Once she'd received tenure, she was positive she'd never have to interview again. But there were some things more important than tenure, and she didn't regret her decision to follow her heart. The idea of starting over was definitely scary, but it was what she had to do.

The office door opened, and Maggie felt immediately welcomed by the dean's quick smile. Following her into the room, Maggie took the seat in front of the desk and looked up expectantly.

"So, tell me something about yourself that isn't on your CV." The dean sat forward in her chair and laced her hands on her desk blotter.

There was only one thing that came to mind, and it had nothing to do with her credentials or her hobbies. She took a deep breath and decided to bite the bullet, believing, despite everything, that honesty was the best policy. "There is something you should know if you want to consider me for this position."

"Oh? Do you have a nefarious past?" There was the hint of a smile at the corner of the dean's mouth.

"What? No, although there are some who may think

otherwise. You see, the reason I'm on the job market is because my current work environment has become a place that isn't comfortable for me any longer."

"In what way?"

Maggie took a deep breath. "Because I'm in a relationship that many of my coworkers disapprove of, and they made that disapproval known to me, as well as to my dean. The trouble has passed now, but I don't feel safe there any longer."

"I see. I only have one question—are we talking inappropriate behavior with a student?"

"It's fully consensual. She's a grad student in her midtwenties, and we met in a class I was teaching, which she subsequently dropped. We are now living together. This didn't sit well with some of my more conservative colleagues."

"That was a very diplomatic way to say busybodies who can't mind their own business. Well, I appreciate your candor, though, quite frankly, it wasn't necessary."

"I wanted the opportunity to tell my own story, because you'd surely hear about this if you contacted my department, and I want to answer any questions you may have." Maggie was surprisingly calm. She realized that her confidence came from the fact that she felt right about the decisions she had made.

"I appreciate that. It's really none of my business, however. You're both consenting adults, she's not an undergraduate, and she's not your student. Will she be coming to school here if you get the job?"

"I'm confident she'd move here with me, but I don't know if she'd transfer to this program."

"I see. Well, just so you know, we have a good group of people here. They do their jobs well and collaborate quite effectively when they need to. And from what I've seen and heard, people live and let live."

Half an hour later, Dean James ended the interview on an encouraging note. "So that you take that long drive with good news, I must tell you I am going to recommend to the search committee that you get the job. I know they are considering other candidates, but I want you at the top of the list. I think you would make a fine addition to the department." She extended her hand across her desk and Maggie shook it gratefully.

❖

Maggie called Rory to recap the interview, and then meandered through campus in search of food before the next phase of the day of interviews. She liked what she saw. This was a place where she and Rory could get a fresh start. They could get a bigger house, with room for all of Rory's books and plenty of space for them both to work. Maybe a place with a backyard so Rory could finally have a dog. This was a place where they could be themselves, where no one would try to put their nose into their business, where no one would try to tell them what they were doing was wrong.

She did feel some trepidation about the prospect of asking Rory to give up on her current program of study and start over in a new school. No matter how much Rory loved her—and she knew instinctually that Rory would follow her anywhere—did she have the right to ask her to do so? But could she patiently wait for Rory to finish her degree? Living apart for that long would be hard on them both, because home was where Rory was, plain and simple.

CHAPTER NINETEEN

S o the second interview went well?"

"I think so. They seemed happy with my answers." Maggie was back in her hotel room later that evening. After the interview with the search committee, the dean had invited her to dinner and they had swapped stories about their careers. She had felt relaxed the whole evening. It hadn't felt as if she was sitting at the table with someone who could very well be her boss in a few months, but, instead, a friend she had known for years. She was more hopeful than ever that she would receive a job offer.

"Baby, I'm glad."

"So, what was your day like today?"

"The usual, read for class, cleaned some, slayed a few dragons, then made dinner for one."

"Oh, my poor baby. Sounds like a tough day." Maggie smiled as she teased her lover.

"It was. You just don't know. Slaying dragons isn't easy, but it had to be done. They were getting mud on the carpet and I had just vacuumed. It was damned inconsiderate."

Maggie laughed. "I hope you didn't get blood everywhere."

"No, no, I know what I'm doing." Rory was silent, then, "I wish you were here next to me."

"I know, baby, me too."

"Where are you right now?" Maggie heard seduction in Rory's soft voice.

"I'm in bed. Contemplating what I can do to make myself fall asleep."

"I have an idea."

Maggie chuckled. "I bet you do."

"I can love you from this far away. Want to see me try?"

Maggie inhaled. "My love, I don't know if what you're proposing is a good idea."

"Why not? Are you afraid you'll get too turned on and won't be able to do anything about it?"

Maggie snuggled down into the pillows, holding the phone close to her, and pulled the covers up. "That's exactly what I'm afraid of."

"I can help you with that. I can tell you exactly where I would be touching you right now if I was there, and you can touch those places for me and close your eyes and imagine me there. Imagine the touch of my lips on your body, my fingers trailing up your leg, the feel of my—"

"Stop," Maggie interjected with a nervous chuckle. "Oh, honey, please don't, that's torture. I only want the real thing. I can't settle for less."

"But I am the real thing."

"Yes, but you're not here. I don't want to imagine you doing those things. I want you doing those things. Does that make sense?"

"It makes perfect sense, my love."

"I'm sorry for ruining your play."

"You didn't. It's not all about me. I want to please you and make you happy, and if you're not into it, that's okay. Besides, I've never done that before, so I probably wouldn't be very good at it."

"Oh, I beg to differ. I think you would have been quite successful." Just from those few exchanges, Maggie had started to get wet, thanks to the seductive quality of Rory's voice as it glided over her body, just as her lips and fingers often did. "You have a very sexy voice when you want to."

"I do?" Rory sounded almost embarrassed.

"Oh, my love, you really do. I love your voice. It's like music."

Rory was silent for a moment. And then she began softly to sing one of the songs Maggie recognized from the playlist.

Maggie smiled contentedly as the words flowed over her. To hear the love in Rory's voice was a perfect way to end her day. But it was still torture when, at the end of the song, she couldn't put her arms around Rory and pull her close. When the song was over, Maggie sat quietly, and Rory did nothing to break the silence. Finally, Maggie said, "You make everything beautiful. I love you so much."

"Except you. You were already beautiful. The most beautiful woman I've ever seen, and I feel so lucky that you see me."

"I'm the lucky one."

"You want me to sing you to sleep, my love?"

"I don't know if you can top that."

"Just wait, I still have a few tricks up my sleeve." With that, Rory proceeded to sing, soft and slow, "When You Say Nothing at All."

This song wrapped itself around Maggie and the feeling of love that washed over her was intoxicating. She relaxed into it and held on to Rory's voice as long as she could, taking it with her into her dreams.

❖

On the drive home, Maggie rocked out to Rory's second iPod playlist, which she had only found that morning: *Songs to Keep Maggie Awake*. When she arrived home, she was worn out from the drive and hoped that Rory wasn't expecting much from her. She just wanted to put her feet up, have a bite to eat, and maybe have Rory give her a back massage, before she fell into her comfy bed with Rory at her side. When she opened the door, she called out, "Rory, you here?"

Rory came in from the kitchen, a dish towel over one shoulder. "Of course I'm here. Where else would I be? Welcome home." She smiled and went to Maggie and gave her a hug and a light kiss. "Take your shoes off, get comfortable, and I'll bring you something to eat if you're hungry."

Maggie smiled at her gratefully. "That sounds wonderful. What's for lunch?"

"I went all fancy—sandwiches and potato chips." Rory grinned.

"That sounds like the best thing ever." After taking her shoes off, Maggie reclined on the couch in Rory's usual fashion of legs stretched out and her feet crossed at the ankles.

As Rory went into the kitchen to get their lunch, she tossed over her shoulder, "Don't fall asleep now. I might have to do unspeakable things to you."

"Okay, just do them quietly." She gave Rory a small smile before putting her head on the back of the couch. Rory disappeared into the kitchen, only to reemerge a moment later with two plates of the promised food. She offered one to Maggie, then sat on the edge of the couch, letting Maggie keep her legs stretched out.

Maggie sat up. "Thank you, baby."

"You're welcome. I think we have to get a dog."

"I'm sorry, what now?"

"We have to get a dog. With you gone, there was no one to

cuddle up to, and when I rolled over, that side of the bed was cold. A dog would solve that problem. Or another woman, but I thought the dog would be an easier sell."

"Um, yes it would. I'll think about it."

"Good. I don't care what kind he is either, I just want him to be whiskey brown so we can call him Tennessee. Not really after the alcohol or the state, but the playwright."

"Of course."

"So, tell me all the things you didn't tell me on the phone."

"What do you mean?"

"You know, what's the campus like, what's your potential new boss like? Would we be happy there?"

"Oh, those things."

"Yeah, those things."

"Well, I think we would. The campus is small but beautiful. The theater department doesn't have as many programs as ours. Only the basics—acting, directing, stage management—but enough for the both of us. I just got a good vibe there, overall. I think we could both be happy." She smiled at Rory and tried to eat the lunch Rory had prepared, even though she was a little too worn out to eat.

"Then I hope this happens for us."

"Rory?"

"Hmm?" Rory asked around a bite of her sandwich.

"I haven't asked how you feel about all this. I'm sorry. I know it probably doesn't seem like it, but I really have been thinking about you too and how a move would affect you. I don't want you to think that I take it for granted that you would just drop everything and follow me wherever I go. I don't expect that, though I would be lying if I said I didn't hope."

Rory didn't speak as she wiped her face with a napkin, then set her plate on the coffee table. She turned to Maggie and said, "I appreciate you saying that. I know it means you respect me as an individual with my own life and my own goals. However, you should know by now that wherever you go, I go. My place is with you. I can get an education anywhere."

Maggie set her plate on the table next to Rory's. "You wouldn't want to finish your degree here and then follow me there, should they hire me?"

Rory scooted closer and took Maggie's hands in both of hers. "Baby, I am an independent girl, who can live on her own, away from my parents, and not feel the need for a roommate. I can cook and clean for myself and pay bills. I can get myself out of bed to go to class, even the early ones, and get my work turned in on time. I can do all of those things, as I've learned how to pretend well at this adulting thing." They shared a smile. "But do you know what I can't do?"

Maggie said nothing, just shook her head no.

"What I can't do, Maggie Parks, is be without you. I don't want to sound all codependent and pathetic, but that's the sad truth. Living without you would hurt me too much. I think I could get used to overnights away now and then—I know the life of an academic means conferences in faraway places and I won't always be able to go with you—but something more than that? No way. And don't go feeling selfish, because you haven't asked me to give up everything and follow you, the way Maxine asked you. What I do, I do of my own free will. Understood?"

Maggie brushed a curl aside and gave Rory a small kiss, then sat back and smiled. "Understood."

"Good. I hope you get this job because I already applied there."

"Do what?"

"Yeah, besides all that dragon slaying I did, I spent most

of the day filling out the application. God, why does every school make that process so freaking long?"

"Wait, wait, wait...you applied to the school I had a job interview with just in case I got the job?"

Grinning, Rory nodded yes.

"Why didn't you tell me?"

Rory threw her hands up in the air. "Surprise!"

Maggie just shook her head and laughed. "And to think, I was worried about how you would take this. So what else did you do that you haven't told me?"

"Well, I did have to bribe some people to write me letters of recommendation, but I strong-armed them into it and was able to get everything sent off. They have rolling admissions, in case you don't know, and I should know by summer. Does that answer your question?"

"Um, yes, I guess it does." Maggie lightly smacked her on the knee. "Sneaky wench."

"And a busy one. I've also taken the liberty of looking for houses to rent within walking distance of the campus."

"You have, have you? I don't suppose you've priced moving companies too?"

"Oh, I've done everything. Even picked out where our children will go to school."

"Have you now?"

"Yes, and it's not far from the house I really like."

"Well that's good. What about your parents?"

"There's a guest room."

"You know what I mean."

Now sounding serious, Rory said, "Yeah. I called them. They were a little surprised, but they understood. They said it's my life and my decision and they will support me either way. Then I told Dad I would be sure to take his gold ducats with me and dress like a boy as I made my escape." Seriousness gone, she grinned.

Maggie laughed at the Shakespeare reference. "Ha-ha. But you are cute when you dress like a boy."

"I always dress like a boy."

"And you're always cute."

"You know what they say about flattery."

"I've already gotten everywhere with you. What's left?"

"True. So tell me what can I do for you in the here and now to please you?"

Maggie sighed. "Get comfortable." Maggie lightly pushed Rory back on the couch, then lay on top of her. Rory put her arms around her, kissed the top of her head, and said nothing more.

Chapter Twenty

They didn't say anything to anyone at first; they wanted to wait until they knew more. But, three weeks later, Maggie was offered the job. The first people they told were Rory's parents.

"Do you know how far a drive that's going to be for us?" Rory's father teased.

"Yes, Dad, I do. It's not that far. Stop your whining."

"I'm your father and a lot older than you. Whining is my prerogative. Besides, it was bad enough losing my baby girl to a lover, now I have to really set her free into the wild. I don't know if I can bear it."

"What wild? I'm going to be in Minnesota. You know, where Laura Ingalls was from?"

"Yeah, I know. In the big woods. They have big woods there. That's wild."

"And a long time ago. I think they've tamed down a bit now."

"You don't know that. How can we trust that? And they have Vikings there. If I ever hear you rooting for the Vikings, you're out of the will."

"See, you keep saying that, but I don't think there even is a will. I think you're just trying to keep me in line with the promise of riches."

"You found me out. I'm really as poor as a church mouse. I've seen selling off the family treasure little by little just to put you through college. At this rate, I'll be too poor to die."

"No problem, I'll just bury you in the backyard."

"Would you? That would be so kind of you."

"Dad, I don't know how to tell you this, but there is one secret Maggie and I haven't told you."

"Can my heart take it?"

"Not sure. You ready?"

"Lay it on me."

"You're going to be a grandpa."

Silence. Then, "Well, congratulations, I guess. This is me, pretending it's not too soon for the two of you to have children."

Giggling now, Rory said, "Too soon? I've wanted a dog since I was a kid, you know that."

"A dog?"

"Yeah, of course. It's way too soon to have children. That's a talk we haven't even had yet, but eventually."

"Aurora Dawn Morgan, the next time you tell me I'm going to be a grandpa, it better be because one of you is in the family way."

"Sorry, Dad."

"No you're not, you spoiled brat. But I'm going to miss you. Don't forget to come home at Christmas."

"We won't. Once we get all settled, you guys should come and visit. Maybe see the wilds of Minnesota for yourself."

"I think your mother and I would like that very much. Rory, just tell me you're happy. That's all we've ever wanted."

"Dad, I have never been happier. This is right for both of us. I got lucky, Dad, I found my true love early. I'm going to do everything I can to hold on to her and be the person she deserves."

"You already are that, my dear. And I can tell how much she cares about you. You're right—you got damn lucky, always remember that. If you can remember how special she is and never forget that she could have had anyone she wanted, but she chose you out of all the others, then you will have a happy life. Never let her forget she's special."

Almost choking up, Rory said, "I won't. Thanks, Dad."

Rory decided to handle the next news delivery in person, so she went to the dorm to talk to Rachel, after verifying that she was in fact home.

While Rory was in the elevator, Rachel texted: *This is your weather report. The skies are shallow, with a chance of petty and bitchy. Proceed with caution.*

Rachel was telling her that she had company. Rory responded: *I'm always prepared. Are you?* She walked down to Rachel's door and knocked. She was in the mood for some fun.

Rachel opened the door and Rory pulled her into a hug. "Oh my God, I've missed you so much. These weeks without seeing you have been torture."

A surprised Rachel returned Rory's hug and whispered, "What are you doing?"

Instead of replying, Rory held Rachel at arm's length. "I need you alone. Please, I have something important to tell you. We need privacy." She eyed the three girls in Rachel's room, who were looking at each other, trying to figure out what to do.

"Okay. You're being weird, but sure." Without taking her eyes off Rory, she said over her shoulder, "Everybody out, I want to get laid."

Rory cocked an eyebrow at her but said nothing to refute the statement. The three girls made their excuses and quickly left.

Rachel stepped aside. "Come on in."

Once the door was closed, Rory shook her head. "Get laid? Really?"

"Hey, I've found it's very effective for clearing a room. Besides, one of these times it's going to be true."

"Sorry to tell you, but today is not that day."

"Typical. So why are you here?"

"Because I missed you?"

"And why is that a question? That should be a given."

"Oh, and it is, my dearest, I have missed you so." Rory grabbed Rachel by the shoulders and pulled her in again in a mock dramatic hug.

Rachel pushed her off. "Don't be a tease and don't overact, it's beneath you."

Rory stepped away from her and pulled out Rachel's desk chair, turned it around, and straddled it. Upon seeing this, Rachel shook her head but said nothing. "What?"

"Nothing. You're just such a butch sometimes."

"You say that like it's a bad thing."

"It's not."

"Then why'd you look at me like that?"

"It's just…why does everything you do have to be so freaking sexy? You make it really hard sometimes." Rachel seemed embarrassed at her admission, and she quickly turned away and went to sit on the floor with her back against the bed, with her feet out in front of her, touching Rory's.

For a moment, Rory wasn't sure whether to respond with gentleness or their usual banter. Then she realized, sometimes the banter had to be set aside. "I'm sorry. I wasn't trying to be."

Rachel laughed. "Did you just seriously apologize for being sexy? Geez, Morgan, you can't apologize for something you can't control. And I wouldn't want you to."

"Okay. I just meant I'm sorry if I had made you uncomfortable."

"It's okay, I'm used to it. The fact of your hotness, I mean." They shared a smile.

"I take no responsibility for that—that's my parents' doing. Besides, you're hot too."

"I don't need your pity."

"It's not pity, you moron, it's the truth. You're a hot, sexy blonde, and someday, you too will find the woman of your dreams and she will appreciate all that you are."

"From your lips to my vagina."

Rachel said it in all seriousness and Rory just stared at her at first before bursting out in laughter. They shared a good belly laugh for a good two minutes. It felt good to laugh like that, Rory thought. It had been a long time for them.

Wiping her eyes, Rory said, "Oh my God, what am I going to do without you?"

"Lucky for you, you won't have to find out. You're not getting rid of me."

"No, but you're getting rid of me."

"What are you talking about?"

"Maggie got a job offer in Minnesota starting in the fall. I'm going with her and, if I get accepted, transferring there."

Rachel didn't say anything for a moment. Then she said, "You're leaving me?"

Rory looked down at the carpet for a moment before meeting Rachel's sad eyes. "I have to follow her, Rach. She's my everything. I'm sorry."

Rachel quickly wiped her eyes and gave a small chuckle. "There you go again, apologizing for something you can't control. I know you have to follow her. I just hate it. I fucking hate it." Rachel kicked at Rory's feet and that's when the real tears fell.

Rory quickly got up from her chair and sat down next to Rachel, putting her arms around her shoulders but saying nothing. Rachel didn't lean her head on Rory's shoulder; instead, she drew her knees up and leaned forward on them. Rory rubbed her back.

Through her tears, Rachel said, "You're my best friend."

"And you're mine. That hasn't changed. I love you, Rachel, I always will."

Finally, wiping her eyes, Rachel sat back and chuckled. "Forgive me. I've had a bad week. I just found out I've been cheated on."

"You were in a relationship?"

"Yeah. Someone I met in class. She asked to keep things on the down low, she said, because she wasn't out yet. I didn't like it but I respected it. Come to find out, she had another girlfriend. Someone on the basketball team. Apparently, they went to high school together, and Jessica, the bitch who lied to me, had never dated anyone else, so she wanted to see what that was like. I was a fucking experiment."

"Aw, I'm sorry, love. Where's this bitch live? I bet I could take her."

"Better send Maggie, at least she has combat skills. You, not so much."

"Hey, I'm told I can be intimidating."

"Really, to who? Short people?"

"That's not nice. And to think, I was going to give you comfort. Well, screw that." Despite her words, she grinned and winked.

"So, anyway, I appreciate you telling me in person."

"Of course."

"Does this mean that you're going to make an honest woman of her someday?"

"Marriage?"

"Yes, marriage. Don't act like you've never heard of it. Why not marriage?"

"I have nothing against it. I just think it might be too soon is all."

"I didn't say you had to take her to the courthouse and marry her before you leave town, but there's no reason why you can't propose."

"Well, no, but why should I do this? I mean, she already knows I love her and that I would obviously follow her anywhere. What purpose would it serve? I don't want her to think I'm rushing things."

Rachel looked at Rory like she'd never seen her before. "What purpose would it serve? Did you really just ask me that? You, the queen of the big romantic gesture? What purpose would it serve? Surely you must be joking."

Rory grinned but refrained from responding with the old joke, and instead said, "No, I'm not. Tell me why I should propose, right now."

"Geez, do I have to think of everything? How about because you love her and you want to spend the rest of your life with her. Do you need a better reason?"

"No, I guess not." Rory looked off into the distance, thinking it over. Finally, "I'm liking the idea of a proposal. I must have a think on this. It should be big."

"Yes, abso-freakin'-lutely. Go big or go home, Morgan. This should be epic. Something befitting the stage."

"Something tells me you already have something in mind."

Rachel's eyes lit up. "I do. Flash mob."

"Flash mob? I'm not really the flash mob type and neither is she."

"That's why it's so perfect, she won't expect it. But you're both theater people and it would be romantic and big and perfect. Think about it…she walks to class like a normal day, the hallway is full of people, like a normal day, then all of a sudden, some awesome song starts playing, so not like a normal day. This makes her wonder. Then, those people in the hall start dancing and they steer her toward the classroom, where you wait to pop the question. It's perfect. Oh my God, this would be so awesome. Let me plan this for you, *please*." Rachel clasped her hands as if in prayer.

"God, you theater people are so dramatic."

"Please."

Rory looked into Rachel's eager face and tried to suppress a smile. "Okay, fine, plan me a flash mob. I don't know how you're going to get Charles to allow this, though."

Rachel stood up. "You call our dean by his first name?" Rory shrugged. "Leave him to me, he likes me, he'll do anything I ask. Let me worry about the details. You worry about more important things, like what you're going to wear."

"I was going to go with clothes."

Rachel sighed and shook her head. "You're impossible."

Maggie headed to the dean's office to break the news to Charles. She had planned to talk to Bill and Dix later, but as fate would have it, Bill was in the dean's outer office. "Well, this is fortunate. I was going to come and see you, but now I can talk to both you and Charles at the same time."

"Uh-oh, sounds serious." He went up to Maggie and kissed her on the cheek. "How you doing, love?"

"Oh, I'm very good, thanks. How's Dix?"

"The usual, whining about how he can't wait for summer to get here, but then, when it does, he'll be whining about how it's too hot to do anything." Bill rolled his eyes and it made Maggie laugh. "How's that young stud of yours?"

Maggie smiled. "Fine. I have much to tell you, follow me to Charles's office."

Suddenly leery, he said, "Why do I get the feeling I should be leaving a trail of breadcrumbs?"

Laughing, Maggie took his hand and led him the few steps to Charles's door. "I think we'll be fine. Come on." She knocked, and when she heard "Come in," they entered together.

Charles looked up from his computer with a weary expression. "I'm not sure I want to know what this is about."

"Well, I do," Bill said. "I have no idea why I'm here."

"Maggie, what's going on? Bullies on the playground again?"

"Not this time. Sit down, Bill."

"Yes, ma'am." Dutifully, Bill sat and looked up at Maggie expectantly as she stood in front of Charles's desk.

She took a deep breath and said to her boss, "You will receive formal notice later, but I wanted to tell you in person that this will be my last semester here. I have accepted another position elsewhere."

"You what?" Bill stood up in shock.

Maggie half turned and held up her hand to him. "Hold on." She turned back to Charles, who hadn't said anything yet. "Charles?"

"I want to say I'm surprised, but I'm not."

"Well, I am!"

Charles looked at Bill. "She already told me that she was having problems staying because of those jerks." He looked at Maggie. "I understand. I hate it, but I understand. Besides, when Rory asked for a letter of recommendation, I knew that you must be serious."

"She asked for one from me too, and you told me about your interview, but I didn't know you had gotten the job. I don't know how I feel about that." Bill looked stunned and Maggie sat beside him and took his hand.

"I'm going to miss you most of all." She grinned and he sneered at her.

"Are you calling me stupid?"

Maggie laughed. She knew he was joking. "No, my dear, I mean it. I *will* miss you most of all."

"Excuse me, I'm right here. The dean who now has to look for a replacement in a flipping hurry. Thanks so much for that."

"Relax, Charles, it's only April. You have four whole months to find someone." She snickered. "I am sorry this is kind of last minute, but I felt I had no other choice."

"I know, I do. I understand. I wish you well." Charles stood up and offered his hand. "It's been a pleasure working with you, Maggie, and I wish you much happiness."

Maggie took his hand and gave him a firm handshake. "Thank you, Charles."

"I'm sorry to lose you. You really are a great teacher."

"Thank you." Before she could say more, she heard Bill crying quietly.

"I don't know what's worse, you leaving, or watching Barbara Hershey die over and over again." Maggie put her arms around him. "You'd better have a well-decorated guest room for us out in Minnesota."

Chapter Twenty-one

On the last day before the beginning of finals, Maggie headed out of her office, locking the door behind her. It was the last class she would teach at this school, and she was already feeling nostalgic about it. She would miss her students here, miss seeing them shine when they found their niche. She would miss watching the students she had known for years as they progressed on their journeys. She only carried her class notes with her. As she started walking down the hallway, she noticed there were a lot of students milling about. Normal for a typical day, but it seemed a lot for the week before finals, since some professors canceled class that week.

Before she could get too far, she heard loud music start up from somewhere. It was a song she knew and liked, one Rory played often: "Love Sneaking Up on You."

Suddenly, the people in the hallway started dancing.

"What the…?"

All of a sudden, everyone in the hallway was dancing, and several of the students shimmied up to Maggie in a way that made her want to join in, and she smiled at them, enjoying the show. After all, this was the theater department. Anything was possible, though a big dance number in the hallway, that was new.

The hallway was full of people now. All the classrooms

had emptied and everyone joined in. Several students flanked her as if to guide her forward, as they kept dancing to the beat. They made their way all the way down the hallway to Maggie's classroom and just as she was about to thank them for the escort, the music changed to another song she recognized: "Home," by Phillip Phillips. But this was no recording; she recognized Rory's voice coming from the classroom and entered the room in amazement. There was Rory, sitting on the teacher's desk, and she was singing to her. When Maggie took another step in, Rory jumped off the desk and walked up to Maggie, still singing.

Rory took both of Maggie's hands in hers as she sang the final lines. Maggie smiled and cried softly at the same time. When the music stopped, Rory started to speak. "Maggie, I just want you to know, I love you so much. I want to make a home for you to come home to. And I want you to know that my place is with you. You are my home." Rory kneeled on one knee and Maggie choked back a sob. Rory produced a ring box. "Margaret Ann Parks, will you do me the honor of being my wife?"

Maggie wiped the tears from her cheeks and nodded, incapable of speech. Rory slipped the ring on her finger, then stood up and put her arms around Maggie, lifting her off the ground. The cheers from the hallway were almost deafening.

All of a sudden, the dean's voice could be heard above the din. "All right, that's enough. Back up, everyone back up." The crowd became quiet and Rory set Maggie back on the ground, and they turned toward the door.

Charles came into the classroom, looking angry. "Margaret, I've got something to say to you."

Maggie stood in front of Rory protectively. "Be careful, Charles."

Charles looked bewildered for a moment. "Be careful?

All I wanted to say was congratulations." He extended his hand, first to Maggie then to Rory, and they shook cautiously. Then he turned to the crowd in the hall. "All right, fun's over. Get back to class." The crowd started to disperse, except for Rachel, who barged in and put her arms around Rory.

"Oh my God, I'm so happy for you, Morgan! I told you it would work."

Rory returned the hug, and then gently extricated herself from Rachel. "Maggie, Rachel was the mastermind behind all this."

"Oh, thank you. This was fabulous."

Rachel blushed then elbowed Rory. "So, I'm totally going to be your person of honor, right? Will I have to wear a dress? What colors do you think you're going to go with?"

Rory put both hands on Rachel's shoulders. "Rachel?"

"Yes, Rory?"

"Go away now. I can take it from here."

"Right." Rachel hooked her arm through the dean's. He looked profoundly shocked by this. "Come on, Charles. We're not wanted here."

"Ms. Cole, what are you doing?"

"Relax, we're just leaving." Rachel waved at Rory and Maggie as she and Charles walked out the door.

Rory and Maggie couldn't help but laugh. Maggie put her arms around Rory's neck. "You sneaky little brat. You got me."

"I hope so. That's why I proposed."

"This was totally different and totally wonderful. I loved it."

"I'm glad."

"I have one question though."

"What's that, my love?"

"Where are my students?"

Rory laughed. "Oh, yeah. I asked Charles to email them

all the review sheet you made and then tell them class was canceled. Are you upset I messed with your class?"

"Not this time. Just don't make a habit of it. The proposal got you a get-out-of-jail-free card."

"As well as my grandmother's ring?"

Maggie looked at the ring. "This was your grandmother's?"

"Yep. Grandma Morgan. She passed it on to me for my wedding, but I don't think it's my style. Besides, I told you, you're a Morgan now. That comes with bling."

"Really? If I had known that, I would have become a Morgan sooner. I love you, Aurora."

"I love you too, Maggie Parks."

"Soon you won't be able to call me that anymore."

"True. You'll be Maggie Morgan. Quite the alliteration."

"No more talking. I think, my lovely one, you need to kiss me now."

"Biased," Rory whispered, as she leaned in for a kiss.

Author's Note

The college where Rory and Maggie meet is not named, nor is its exact location, because it only exists in my imagination. I borrowed bits and pieces from all the colleges I've attended to make one homogenous whole.

Likewise, the Minnesota college Maggie and Rory are headed to does not exist in Minnesota but is a tribute to my undergrad alma mater in a different state, a school to which I owe a great debt, in more ways than one.

Early on in the process of writing this novel, I met a lovely young woman on the bus. We often rode it at the same time and would fall into conversation, but, alas, I have an incredible ability for forgetting people's names and so would often forget hers. In an effort to remember it, I created a minor character and gave her that young woman's name. I hope she will indeed read the book, as she said she would, and will enjoy seeing her name, no matter how briefly.

The characters in this book are all products of my imagination, but I borrowed a few names to honor some of my friends who have been supportive and encouraging throughout this process. I hope they know how I appreciate each and every one of them.

And if you're wondering if there was ever a Maggie in my life, the answer is no, though I had my share of teacher crushes in my day. Unlike Rory, I was never brave enough to ask any of them out. I'm sure the loss was wholly my own.

About the Author

An Illinois transplant, Ms. Hayes is a recent graduate of the master's program in educational studies at the University of Oklahoma. She also holds a master's degree in English from Western Illinois University. She professes no specific title, even the Ms. is somewhat of a misnomer, as she does not personally ascribe to any particular gender, but is legally still considered a female, as there is not yet a "None of the Above" option. She resides (rather uncomfortably, both politically and climatically) in Oklahoma, with her transgender husband Jaykob, whom she has not yet legally married. This is her first novel.

Lightning Source UK Ltd.
Milton Keynes UK
UKOW02f0928020816

279755UK00001B/45/P